"W... sabotage the ButterCup?

Joy hated it when Rain's voice took on that sarcastic tone. "As if you didn't know!" she burst out. "Do you honestly believe all those people lined up for cruises are there for the houseboat?"

"And not for the free steak? Instead of asparagus quiche at the ButterCup—is that what you're saying?"

"Yes," Joy had to admit. "That's what I'm saying."

"Can you prove they're not?"

She was taken aback. "Well, no. I mean, how—"

"Precisely. Maybe I should stand on the gangplank and ask. Sir? Madam? What are your intentions? Honorable or otherwise?"

Joy sat in miserable silence, her arms wrapped around her knees. It was hopeless; they were back at square one.

"Listen." Rain gently caught her hand and pressed a kiss into the palm. "There *is* a solution," he murmured. "Every good impasse has one."

Monica Martin grew up in a pioneer setting in the Laurentian Mountains of Quebec, the landscape she evokes so effectively in *The ButterCup Dream*. She now lives on a farm near London, Ontario, with her husband, a cat and a part-time dog (really her daughter's). Both her children are grown, leaving Monica with lots of time for writing romances—and for cooking, gardening and music, pleasures which all seem to find their way into her stories!

The ButterCup Dream

Monica Martin

Harlequin Books

**TORONTO • NEW YORK • LONDON
AMSTERDAM • PARIS • SYDNEY • HAMBURG
STOCKHOLM • ATHENS • TOKYO • MILAN**

ISBN 0-373-02908-X

Harlequin Romance first edition May 1988
Second printing May 1988

CHAPTER ONE

IT WAS THE KIND of June morning when the whole world seemed to be running perfectly. The first hint Joy Lowry had that it wasn't came when the truck from Raymond Frères Lumberyard pulled up across the road and started unloading two-by-fours onto the beach.

She was in the kitchen at the time. A pleasantly curved small figure in jeans and a yellow sweatshirt marked ButterCup Café, she was having an early coffee and rolling out pastry shells while JS purred around her legs making the usual nuisance of himself. Her light brown eyes were thoughtful between thick straight fair lashes. Asparagus maybe, instead of mushroom quiches for tomorrow's grand opening, even though it meant she'd have to rewrite the menu. She had seen some at the market yesterday and she liked the idea of using local produce in season. Usually she had the radio on, tuned to Bach or Vivaldi if she could find them, but this morning there was a robin singing in the lilacs and she had simply opened the window wide. Amazing, the amount of music in the country! It was only three months since she'd bought the cottage in the Québec Laurentians with the idea of turning it into a café, and the whole thing still felt like a dream come true.

When grinding gears, followed by shouts and the clash of timber, drowned out the robin, she picked up her coffee cup and went out on the porch to look.

Sunlight danced on the water, and all around the lake the mountains thrust shaggy green heads into an azure sky. Across the road, two men from the lumberyard were stacking boards on the sand. For a moment she thought she was seeing things. Already the pile was high enough to blot out half the little town of Lac Désir du Coeur, nestled amid the birches across the bay. As if she didn't already have enough to worry about! It had to be a mistake; that was the only explanation. She set her cup on the railing and marched across the road, rehearsing the French word for mistake.

"¡Allô! You must have the wrong place. ¡Une erreur!"

The men straightened, staring. She wasn't tall, and her hair was an uncombed halo of springy gold curls, but she had what her aunt used to call presence. The younger man grinned.

"No mistake, Mademoiselle Lowry. This is the place."

"But it's a beach. Sand. Nobody lives here."

"The directions are on the invoice."

She hesitated, at a loss. "Is there a name?"

"No. Paid in cash." He winked. "You want to see?"

"Non, merci." She stepped back. The local teen heartthrob; she'd dealt with him once at the lumberyard. That time, he had tried to interest her in some pine paneling at the back of the shed.

She watched them start sliding twenty-foot logs from the truck, then trailed uncertainly back to the cottage. Now what? She'd have to call someone. She discarded Raymond Frères and the police for the time being and thought of Clémence LeClair. "Call me if there's a problem," the real estate agent had said, in her smoky sympathetic voice. "Anytime. I'll leave you my home number."

She looked it up on the list tacked over the reception desk and dialed. She liked Clémence—who also happened to be related to half the town's population. If anyone knew what was going on, she did. It was dim and cool in the little wainscotted foyer. The fresh smell of wax mingled with the cinnamon scent of sweet williams in an earthenware jug. When Clémence answered after six rings, Joy could tell she'd been asleep. She felt a twinge of guilt.

"I'm sorry! This is Joy speaking. I forgot it's only 8:15."

"Ah, *bonjour*, Joy. No matter!" Clémence yawned and switched to huskily accented English. "How are things at the ButterCup this fine morning?"

"That's why I'm calling. There's a truck from Raymond Frères delivering lumber on the beach, of all places. I wondered if you knew anything."

"Strange, not a thing. What kind of lumber?"

"Building materials. Boards, logs. Didn't you tell me the beach is owned by somebody in British Columbia?"

"The MacCallum boy, *oui*." Joy heard the click of a cigarette lighter and an indrawn breath as Clémence came alive. "The beach and your cottage originally belonged together. When the older MacCallums passed away, the son split up the property. He sold the cottage and moved out west. That was, oh, five years ago."

"Maybe he sold the beach, too, in the meantime. Or else it's squatters," Joy suggested, with all kinds of disturbing prospects opening up before her. She ran a distracted hand through her hair. "Clémence, I had that bow window in the dining room installed specially. And the side porch glassed in and screened. I sat up nights sewing valances and ate supper at all eight tables to make sure every diner could see the sunset. The last thing I need is somebody blocking the view with a big ugly two-story condominium."

Clémence chuckled. "How wide is the beach? Forty feet? Lac Désir may be small, but we do have building regulations. *Calme-toi, ma petite.* I will find out what is going on."

"Would you?"

"Give me half an hour to have my coffee and do my face. Joseph Raymond is an old beau of mine."

"Clémence, you're an angel."

She put down the receiver, wishing she felt as reassured as she sounded. Staring up at her from this week's edition of the *Lac Désir News* was a color photo of the cedar-shingled cottage reclining comfortably on its mossy old lawn.

"New restaurant heralds start of tourist season," read the caption. Farther down the page was a picture of her face, looking eager and young and oh, so optimistic—a look that had to be the fault of her cupid's-bow upper lip, she decided, and the way it ended on either side in dimpled indentations. "Owner and chef, Joy Lowry, to offer light dining in a rustic setting with unmatched view of the lake."

She sighed; she'd be lucky if the "unmatched" didn't turn out to be poetic license. She moved between the freshly scrubbed pine tables in the dining room and gazed uneasily out of the window at the beach. The men were heaving a keg of nails and half a dozen bags of cement down from the truck. Under the window another blossom was opening in the fretwork planter; at least the geraniums and baby's breath were doing their best.

She simply couldn't afford any unexpected problems. The café would have to start paying for itself, fast. Renovations and equipment had gobbled up her nest egg at an alarming rate and the next mortgage payment was due in a week. Brian Upshaw had warned her that her budget was too tight.

"Inside of a year you'll be back. Begging for your old desk at Lloyd & Upshaw's," he predicted. "I know the pattern of these shoestring ventures. On top of which, you've got other strikes against you." He had ticked them off on manicured white fingers. "A woman on her own, no experience, a remote location." He should know, he and his partner specialized in small-business law. All the same, she'd felt compelled to argue her case. He had retreated behind his mahogany desk, elegant face stiff and pale. "And our friendship? The fact that I hoped it could someday be something more? I take it you're willing to throw all that away."

"I had hoped you wouldn't see it like that, Brian. Your friendship is important to me. Right now more than ever—"

"But not important enough to make you stay?"

She hadn't answered that; she hadn't wanted to hurt him. When the staff threw a farewell dinner for her, he was out of town. She hadn't heard from him since her move.

As she watched the truck from the lumberyard spinning its tires in the sand, she reflected that she hadn't even told Brian the worst of it. The day before she signed the mortgage, there had been a second offer for the cottage and she'd been obliged to go $3000 higher than she'd intended—money that was to have been her cushion till the café established itself.

The truck disappeared around a bend in a cloud of dust. Ruts crisscrossed the parts of the beach not covered with lumber. The sun glinted on a couple of soft-drink cans that hadn't been there earlier, and the blue flag iris under the birch tree was trampled flat. Anger mixed with the gnawing sense of apprehension in her mind. She went back to the kitchen and thrust the quiche shells into the fridge and banged open the lid of the stock pot simmering on the rear burner. With an effort she relaxed the frown on her brow. In an hour or so, Clémence would no doubt call and explain the whole thing away with one of her amusing stories of local mixups. Meanwhile, she definitely had to do something about the stock. "More parsley," she decided, putting down the tasting spoon.

She took a deep calming breath of lilac-scented air. The parsley was just beginning to spread nicely in the garden she'd planted by the back door. She bent to pick some and noticed JS, striped like a tiger in the shadows, stalking a robin. She hated it when he caught things; a mouse with tiny pale paws like hands, once even a bird. His back suddenly arched and he froze. Steps pounded over the flagstones.

Something white with enormous jaws hurled itself over the tomato plants. Joy screamed. JS streaked across the lawn and she snatched the screen door open for him just in time. Panting, his attacker slid to a halt. He was a bull terrier with a low-slung muscular frame and grinning piggy eyes.

"Get away! Go home!" she admonished.

The dog ducked his head, shame-faced. Her adrenaline was flowing and she seized him by the collar and marched him around to the front of the cottage. He obviously belonged to somebody in the area; an expensive animal like this hadn't just dropped out of the sky. She didn't have far to look.

"Well, hello. I see Grabber has beaten me to it and introduced himself."

The owner of the baritone stood on the porch, his face shadowy behind the morning glory vine, denim shoulder propping up the doorjamb. Evidently he'd been knocking. Wagging his tail, the dog loped up the steps to join the man.

"Grabber!" Joy echoed. "Good name for a dog that eats cats. Doesn't he come with a leash?"

"Nope. Grabber doesn't like this to be generally known, but his bark's worse than his bite."

"Oh, really? It wasn't his bark that nearly did JS out of one of his nine lives."

"JS?"

"Johann Sebastian." Let him figure it out. "*And* flattened my tomato plants."

"Bach," he stated. "Remind me to buy you a bushel." Coffee-brown eyes rich with humor met hers as she came up the steps. She registered a short brown beard, a wealth of windblown hair, blue jeans that had done hard labor. Parked in the gravel lot was a pickup truck with bruised fenders and a patina of dust.

He was big, all legs and shoulders. And those eyes, trained on her and cheerfully assessing what they saw.

"Five foot three. Hundred and fourteen pounds," she snapped. "I assume you're here for some other reason than exercising your dog and gathering statistics?"

He laughed, drawing the sound all the way up from his boot soles. "Six foot two. Hundred and eighty-five pounds wet. Aren't you going to ask me inside?"

"Should I?"

His eyes dropped to the front of her sweatshirt. "This is the ButterCup Café, isn't it?"

She felt her cheeks redden; that was the trouble with fair skin. The sweatshirt had been her friend Gipsy's idea. Gipsy Connors was a part-time model with television aspirations who could be counted on for clothing that called attention to the wearer.

"If you'd read the sign out front," she said primly, "you'd know we don't open till tomorrow."

"That's okay. Don't apologize. A sandwich and a coffee will do fine."

"You're not listening. We're not serving anything today. If you'll remove your dog, I've got work to finish."

"So have I. But it's hard on an empty stomach." He motioned Grabber to the side, swung open the front door, and followed her inside. "Take-out will do."

"We don't have take-out. Even when we're open." She spun around. "Don't you understand? The café is closed. Take your truck and your dog and go to Lac Désir. They've got a lunch counter on rue Principale, Le Casse-Croûte, that dishes up hamburgers and *patates frites* with gravy and coffee strong enough to float a spoon. In addition, the waitress is cute."

She had no idea why she'd added that last bit. Something to do with the way he stood close to her, tall and male and very much at ease. Something to do with the way his eyes were twinkling. . . .

He heaved a sigh. "I've been eating at truck stops for four days. I was sort of hoping to get away from french fries and gravy."

She made her face uncaring. "Then you'll just have to starve until tomorrow."

"Mind if I look around?" he asked, beginning to do just that. "See what I'm missing?"

A fleeting panic gripped her. The man was a total stranger. "I really am very busy—"

"Go ahead. I won't steal the silver if that's what you're thinking."

"Thanks for the assurance," she said and marched into the kitchen. She retrieved the parsley from the back step and started chopping with a vengeance. If she was going to get nervous about every man who came in, she shouldn't be running a café. Lone men were another risk Brian had warned her about. She listened as he moved through the dining room, his big work boots sounding self-assured and surprisingly light on the maple floor. Three minutes she'd give him, not a second more; after that she'd reach for the phone.

"Nice," he called out. "I like the changes. The bow window. The stuccoed walls. Glassing in the old side porch to make a sun room. Must have cost a bundle. Were they your own ideas, or a decorator's?"

She frowned. "My own. Are you familiar with the cottage?"

He gave a comfortable masculine chuckle. She heard him stop in the doorway to the office. "You might say that. Who's the disapproving-looking gent in the granny glasses and too-tight collar? Boyfriend?"

She crossed the slate floor and fixed him with a disapproving look of her own. The office opened into the kitchen as well as the dining room. It had been a pantry before she'd had the window that faced the garden enlarged, hung some ivy and added a desk and a filing cabinet. "Certainly not. My bank manager, Monsieur Thierry. His picture happened to be in the shareholders' report. I got a few copies and put them up around the cottage as, well, as incentive. Is there anything else you'd like to know?''

''And those are your mortgage payments, I take it, circled in red on the calendar? Three months down and a lifetime to go.''

''Not quite. I saved up, and I inherited some money from a very dear aunt. Not that it's any of your business.''

''No. But it's a relief.'' His big hand came up and lightly brushed the front of her halo. ''Flour. I thought you were already going gray. Listen,'' he said as she drew back a step, ''I'm on your side. I'm in business myself. I know it takes guts. Know-how.'' He nodded at the cookbooks lining the shelves, the neatly-hand-printed menus on the desk. ''Most of all, it takes stamina.''

She smiled in spite of herself. ''You mean it goes on like this? I thought the worst was over.'' He returned her smile with some to spare. He had firm full lips and even, white teeth, and he radiated an easy vitality that made her want to keep on talking to him. ''I mean the plumbing had to be all redone. Another washroom added, and new wiring. Then the front wall almost collapsed when they put in the bow window.'' Her voice trailed away; she seemed to be having trouble disengaging her eyes from his. She heard herself say, ''But that's ancient history now. I could make us a coffee. If you wouldn't mind having it in the kitchen.''

''Mind? I thought you'd never ask.''

He liked what she'd done with the kitchen, too. While she measured the grounds and plugged in the coffee maker, he admired the ceramic wall tiles, the herbs and spices handy on their pine racks, the table with its window seat cushioned in bright marmalade tones. He stretched out long blue-jeaned legs and to her surprise, JS rubbed himself purring against them. "I don't even know your name," she said accusingly.

"I know yours. Joy Lowry."

He could hardly help knowing; it was on ButterCup posters all over town. "And yours?" she prompted.

"MacCallum," he said. "Rain MacCallum."

Her eyes widened. "The MacCallum who owns the beach? Who used to own this cottage and went out west?"

"The same." He held out his hand. "Clémence is still in fine form, I see."

She poured coffee into pottery mugs and ignored the hand. "Yes," she said curtly.

"I think I liked it better when we were strangers. You don't care for neighbors?"

"Not when they come with a truckload of lumber."

His grin was conspiratorial. "You noticed."

"How could I not notice?" She thumped his mug down in front of him and pushed sugar and cream across the table. "I was hoping it was some kind of mistake. It's not?"

"Nope." He helped himself to sugar. "I plan to settle down here. Invest my earnings in the province of Québec."

"But that's a beach you're on. Sand! Maybe you've been away too long. Lac Désir has building regulations now."

"A good thing, too. It's a charming place and we don't want it ruined with irresponsible development, do we?"

"You're laughing at me. I'm serious..."

"And upset." He looked at her with interest. "Did you know that when you're upset, your freckles stand out?"

"I don't have freckles. Only one or two. Come here." She snatched at his sleeve. "Look for yourself. You'll see why I'm upset." She pulled him into the dining room and pointed at the window. "This morning Lac Désir was right across the bay. What do you see now? Yesterday, people would have driven miles for a lunch with that view. Look at it now! And you haven't even started building yet. I know what you do with the beach is none of my business, but I never dreamed—I mean, I bought the cottage in good faith..."

"Mother always said it should have been built farther back, on the hill," he said amiably. "But Dad didn't want all that snow to shovel in the winter."

"My diners will be lucky to see the top of the mountains, once you put up your—retirement home. Or fish plant. Or boat factory—what do I know?"

He looked down at her. The top of her head reached no higher than his shoulder. His voice was soft. "Whatever gave you crazy ideas like that? I'm building a wharf. A dock for my boat."

She expelled a long breath. "That's all? A wharf? A thin, flat, low-in-the-water wharf?"

He shrugged. "It's only a beach. Sand."

She laughed, light-headed with relief. Over her shoulder she said, "Come on, I'll make us a sandwich to go with the coffee. I've got some Black Forest ham."

"On caraway rye? Mustard and lettuce?"

"Of course."

"I have a better idea." He caught up to her with his quick light step and placed a hand on her shoulder, so

casually that she left it there. "I'll make the sandwiches. You finish your parsley."

He made two double-decker sandwiches and they sat
down opposite each other with fresh mugs of coffee.
The stock was going to be the best ever, she could tell by
the aroma. The daisy clock above the counter said
10:15, so she might as well have a break now and work
through lunch. She felt as though she'd known him for
years.

"Of course, I realize people don't build on beaches,"
she said. "It must be all this new responsibility. Knowing what's at stake. It's made me paranoid."

"Not at all. I find your concern quite . . . charming."
He leaned forward and flicked a speck of parsley from
her cheek. He had deft fingers for so large a hand.

"Rain," she said, turning a warm pink. "What an
odd name. Is it short for something?"

"Rainier. My mother's maiden name." He shrugged.
"A bit formal for a guy who makes his living with a
hammer and saw. So I shortened it."

"Is your mother the one who taught you how to
make sandwiches like this?"

"I'm not married, if that's what you're asking."
Under the mustache, it was hard to tell whether he was
smiling. He looked at the pines sunning themselves on
the hill, as though considering the subject. "Moved
around too much, I guess, for any girl to catch me. First
job I had was as a cook at a hunting lodge up north. I
was eighteen."

"You already knew how to cook then?"

He grinned. "No. But I had a week to learn, before
the bush plane was due back."

She wondered how old he was now. Twenty-nine or
thirty perhaps; enough time for laughter to have made

those sun-tanned creases at the corners of his eyes. "After Mom died, I worked my way out west," he was saying. "Cashed in on the building boom. Built up a business of my own."

"And now you've come home—" She caught herself. The cottage was his home, only it belonged to her now; an odd feeling it must be for him.

He gave her a wry look, noting her embarrassment. "Home to Lac Désir, at least," he said smoothly, and finished his sandwich. Whatever his thoughts on the changes that had occurred, he was keeping them to himself. "Let's talk about you instead. What's a Montréal girl like you doing in a place like this?"

"Is it that obvious?" She laughed, glad to change the subject. "I used to spend summers here with my aunt. We stayed at l'Auberge des Vents on the hill. It's closed now. Do you remember it?"

He nodded and she went on. "Every September when we had to go back to the city, I used to cry." She smiled, crinkling her nose at the little girl she used to be. "When I grew up, I realized there was something I could do about it."

His glance shifted back to the pines. "I knew a girl out west who had eyes the color of yours. Butterscotch." He crossed his arms on the table and leaned forward. "Tell me, why a café?"

She lowered her lashes. Butterscotch eyes! She wasn't used to talking about herself, except with Gipsy who was usually too wrapped up in her latest love affair to pay attention. The only family she had left was her father somewhere in California, and she hadn't seen him in years. Brian Upshaw had been interested in her only insofar as she fit in with his plans; she knew that now. The man across the table smiled encouragement as though he could read all this in her mind. Hesitantly she said, "A café seemed natural to me. Something I could do on my own. I love cooking and creating an atmosphere. Making people feel good."

"I can believe that," he said quietly.

He helped her carry the plates and mugs to the sink. He told her he had an appointment with some men he wanted to hire to help him build the wharf. She walked with him to the front door; it was almost as though she was sorry to see him go.

"Where is your boat now?"

"I had it shipped by rail from British Columbia." He stopped in front of the sweet williams shedding their dusky glow. "My mother planted those, years ago." A distant look came into his eyes. "She loved this house. We didn't have much in those days. My father did his best, but jobs tend to be seasonal here in Lac Désir. But when I came home from school, Mom always had flowers on the table and something good in the oven. She made this place a home I wouldn't have traded for a mansion."

"Yet you left—"

"I had no choice. Not if I wanted more from life than my father had." He frowned, back in the present again. "It's only fair to warn you. Building the wharf will mean a couple of days' noise. Lots of coming and going. We'll be starting early and finishing late."

She smiled. "I can live with that. Now that I know it's only a wharf."

"The workmen will need to use your parking lot, too."

"As long as they leave room for my diners."

"What if your diners don't materialize? Not in sufficient numbers to keep Monsieur Thierry happy?"

"I'll manage."

"What if you can't? Have you got somebody to back you up? Family? A boyfriend?"

She shook her head. This was the second time he'd probed about a boyfriend—or about the state of her finances. "It's my own show, Mr. MacCallum. I worked for five years in a Montréal law office. In front of a word processor in a room without windows on the twenty-first floor. There's no way I'm going to let the ButterCup fail."

Light danced in his eyes. "A bit young, aren't you, for all that determination?"

She stood very straight. "I'm twenty-four. Twenty-five in September. I don't think that's too young."

His gaze worked downward, seeking the curves under her sweatshirt. "Not for most things. No." He grinned. "Well, if you change your mind or run into trouble, you can always sell."

"Sell!" She laughed. "Not for a million. I was lucky to get the place. Another buyer—"

"Bid three thousand dollars higher."

She stared and then it dawned on her. "That was you?"

"My lawyer. Yes. I would have gone even higher, but it was too late. You'd matched my three thousand and they'd accepted your offer."

The implications dismayed her. "I suppose that means you're . . . still interested."

"Oh, I'm interested. You know something, Miss Lowry?" He bent down, his eyes roguish, and kissed her on the cheek. "I think I'm going to enjoy being your neighbor."

He was gone before she could react, through the door and down the porch steps with a whistle that brought

Grabber prancing to heel. She brought up a hand to touch her cheek. It still tingled from the silky bristles of his mustache. It took her a moment to realize the telephone was ringing.

"ButterCup Café, good morning," she said, practicing.

Clémence LeClair gave a throaty chuckle. "Listen, *ma petite*, wait till you hear who is back in town."

"I know. He just left here."

"The MacCallum boy? He was there?"

"He's hardly a boy anymore. Yes, he was here. We had coffee and he made sandwiches. He told me he's the buyer who nearly outbid me and he says he still wants to buy the cottage if I want to sell."

"*Mon dieu*. That must have been some *tête-à-tête*. He is...good-looking?" Clémence enquired innocently.

"I suppose...yes. Tall, with a beard. And eyes—" She stopped in disgust; in a minute she'd be sounding like a teenager describing a pop star. "Well, you'll see him for yourself around town."

"What did you tell him? About selling?"

"Clémence!" If anyone knew what the cottage meant to her, it was Clémence. "You have to ask?"

"Only because I was talking to the Raymonds. About the lumber..."

"Oh, that! For the wharf. I heard all about it." She laughed and reached for the stool. "I feel so silly, imagining all those things. Actually, a wharf and a boat might look quite picturesque out there."

Clémence coughed on her cigarette. "Rain MacCallum did not tell you what kind of boat it is?"

"Just a boat. How many kinds are there?"

"A houseboat. The floating circus kind, from what I hear."

Joy's heart dipped painfully in her chest. "A house-boat? To live in?"

"*Oui*. Two stories high, not counting masts, smoke-stack, flagpole and observation deck. Green as a frog. He not only lives in it, he built it. Building custom houseboats is his business and this one is a demonstration model. They say his company is a big success out west."

Why hadn't he stayed out there? She couldn't believe what she was hearing. "Who says? How do you know all this? Has somebody seen the boat?"

"Not yet. The station master at Lac Désir received a message from the railway station down the line. Apparently it is touch and go through the underpasses."

"Well." Joy slid decisively from the stool. "Thanks for the detective work. I'm running late this morning, so I'd better get back to the kitchen." It wasn't Clémence's fault, but if she heard another word about Rain MacCallum or his houseboat, she was going to scream.

The realtor understood. "Do not despair, *ma petite*. Chances are your diners will find the houseboat quite *gai et charmant*."

Joy told her goodbye and hung up. Gay and charming were a lot to hope for. It sounded more like a beached whale. The houseboats she'd seen on television had laundry strung between their masts and used rubber tires as bumpers. Rain MacCallum probably had a stereo that only played rock—single men always did—and gave all-night parties. Heaven only knew what being a demonstration-model houseboat involved. He'd warned her about noise and parking problems but aside from that, he hadn't said a single, solitary word.

"Snake-in-the-grass!" she hissed. JS, lovingly charting the flight of a yellow butterfly through the screen, glanced up in alarm.

"Not you. Rain MacCallum."

She strained the stock and poured most of it into containers for freezing, before leafing through her recipe file to choose tomorrow's soup of the day. Something called a printanière caught her eye, a spring vegetable soup that could be nicely garnished with fresh chives. Somehow, visualizing her choice didn't give her the customary lift. The image of a two-story frog-green houseboat kept intruding. On top of that, she sensed she had the makings of an even bigger problem.

Here she'd spent barely half a morning with an absolute stranger, and already he had the power to make her feel as though she'd been personally betrayed. Things could get a lot worse once he started living right across the road from her.

CHAPTER TWO

JOY FOUGHT HER WAY groggily up from the pillow.

The eggbeater she had been using in her dream had just turned into a roaring chainsaw, sending a blizzard of egg white swirling about her head.

The noise came from outside. It was still dark. She hadn't closed the vertical blinds on the balcony door and a faint glow of light filtered up through the railing from the direction of the beach. Rain MacCallum—who else? She focused sleep-heavy eyes on the clock on her nighttable. Five past five. He'd said early but this was the middle of the night. She fell back with a groan.

The chainsaw whined on and on. She buried her head under the pillow but it didn't help. The bedroom acted like some kind of echo chamber. She flung pillow and duvet aside and staggered across the room.

The balcony floor was rough and cold under the soles of her bare feet. He had rigged a gas lantern up on a pole stuck in the sand and was working in a misty halo of light, a tall muscular figure in jeans and sweatshirt, tousled hair glinting copper. He was sawing two-by-fours into pieces and restacking them. He looked like a man who was enjoying himself. She couldn't see the lake at all, only a dark plain with a white blur that had to be Grabber nosing at the edge of it. Etched in black velvet against the pale band of the horizon were the humped shapes of the mountains. She leaned her elbows on the railing and waited till the saw idled.

"Rain MacCallum! Have you any idea what time it is?"

The circle of light caught his upturned face, throwing the masculine contours into bold relief. His eyes found her on the balcony and a flicker of response ran through her stomach.

"'Morning, neighbor!"

"It isn't! It's night! And there must be a law against what you're doing."

"What? Honest labor?"

"Disturbing the peace! People *were* sleeping."

"Your big opening today. I thought you'd be up by now, sautéing. Basting and garnishing."

She thought of the quiche filling waiting to be made, the maple charlotte russe for tonight, maybe a batch of hermits to put out with coffee, on the house, and wondered if he might not have a point. She drew herself up. "I've got everything under control."

"Glad to hear it. If you're making coffee, I sure could use a cup."

"I'm not." The nerve. "Let's get this straight from the start. The ButterCup does not serve breakfast."

"I'm not asking for ham and eggs. A simple coffee will do."

"Then you'll just have to hold out a while longer. Till your boat gets here and you can make all the coffee and fry all the eggs you want in your glorified galley. Or whatever you call it."

"Oho!" His laughter came rollicking over the railing in a warm good-natured tide. "The Lac Désir grapevine's been at work, has it?"

"Telling me you're building a wharf. Never mentioning that your boat is some kind of... of homemade floating high rise. It slipped your mind, I suppose?"

He swept her a bow. "Mademoiselle Lowry, you are the first one invited across the gangplank when she docks."

"Keep your invitation. If you ask me, houseboats are just a sneaky way for people to live on beaches where they can't build."

"It's only for the summer."

"The summer?"

"You don't expect a man to spend the Canadian winter frozen into the ice on a houseboat, do you?"

Alarm bells rang in her mind. She had forgotten that come October, his need for a land-bound house would be a matter of survival. "If you still think I might cop out and sell you the cottage, forget it."

"Did I mention the word?" His tone was aggrieved. "A man would have to be crazy to rid himself of a neighbor who appears on her balcony arrayed like a vestal virgin."

She drew back with a gasp. She'd been so absorbed, she hadn't realized how rapidly it was growing light. The filmy wisp of nylon and lace she wore scarcely qualified as a nightgown, much less public apparel. "Men!" she hurled down at him, and ducked between the doors.

His voice floated up to her. "Three sugars and plenty of cream!"

The chainsaw leaped and buzzed to cover her answer. She slid the door shut and twitched the blinds tight to hide the rosy flush staining the sky. She looked at the rumpled bed but decided against it. Even if the noise let her sleep, exasperation and—she hated to admit it—the restless excitement generated by their exchange would see to it that she didn't.

THE INCIDENT NAGGED at Joy all morning. It wasn't like her to refuse so basic a request as breakfast to a neighbor. On the other hand, Rain certainly wasn't behaving like the average man next door. So why did her conscience still bother her? She wondered if she might be coming down with something. Most likely, she decided, it was due to lack of sleep.

JS butted an affectionate head against her arm. He didn't care one way or another as they shared a late breakfast, sitting together on the back step. He was interested only in her granola. The robins, Mr. and Mrs., were flying beakloads of hay into the lilacs, and the tomato plants were making a comeback. She told herself she'd chosen the step, instead of her usual table in the sun room, to escape the full brunt of the chainsaw noise; in reality, it was so she wouldn't have to look at what Rain was doing to the beach.

She switched her thoughts to the maple charlotte, nicely chilling in the refrigerator, and the asparagus quiches ready to be popped into the oven. She had worked nonstop since the chainsaw woke her; now, when it whined to a stop, she felt light-headed with relief. Too soon. A truck careened into her parking lot. She leaned over the back gate, which she was keeping shut to prevent any more commando raids by Grabber, and watched two men in work-clothes unload a portable cement-mixer. Rain came to help and they handed him a carton from Le Casse-Croûte. At least now she could stop feeling guilty about breakfast.

By ten-thirty the cement mixer had joined the chainsaw and she almost didn't hear the rapping on the kitchen door. She looked up from the raisins she was adding to the hermit dough to see a reproachful bony face behind the screen.

"Uh, Madame Hebert, is it? Come in...I'm so glad—"

"Surely you are not expecting people to eat with noise like that?"

Although Agnès Hebert came highly recommended by Clémence as a kitchen assistant, it was Joy's first encounter with her steely stare. "Terrible, isn't it? I'm hoping the men will stop over lunch." She hurried the woman through a tour of the dining room and kitchen before leaving her in charge of the salads; she was rewarded with a sniff that might have signified either approval or disapproval. Madame Hebert was obviously not the type to waste words. Just as well. The racket across the road was growing louder, if possible, and the dairy truck hadn't arrived with her order.

Three calls from her office managed to track down the driver. No, he hadn't forgotten the café, and yes, he had the whipping cream. She set the pine tables with flower-sprigged yellow mats and gleaming flatware. The peach napkins in the tall-stemmed wineglasses looked like blossoms; she paused to admire the effect. The sun had reached around to the sun room and she adjusted the bamboo blinds before setting the three tables in there. The fragrance of peonies wafted through the screens. A perfect setting for a romantic luncheon. Or it would have been, if it weren't for Rain and his crew. Another vehicle pulled into her lot and she frowned at it, on principle. But it turned out to be the florist, bounding up the steps with an enormous tissue-wrapped package.

"Best wishes, Brian," was all it said on the card. Well, that was something, considering the way he felt about the café. She tried the arrangement on the pine sideboard but the stiffly formal scarlet and white carnations clashed with the soft natural tones of the décor. She left the vase in the office, holding down a sheaf of invoices.

Back in the kitchen, Madame Hebert surprised her by having the salads completed exactly to specifications. Ruler-straight hips swathed in a white apron, she was washing the morning's accumulation of pots and utensils. Joy breathed a sigh of gratitude for this treasure of initiative, and slipped upstairs to change.

Like Cinderella for the ball, she thought, changing into black chino slacks and an open-necked white shirt and studying her reflection in the closet-door mirror. Black definitely had a slenderizing effect on the hips. And did nice things for fair hair, she noted, knotting a black silk scarf around her neck to complete the café look. She added lipstick and debated for all of three seconds about other makeup, but decided against it. Nothing seemed to have much effect on her scrubbed wholesome look; too bad if some men noticed a freckle here and there. She leaned closer to the mirror. Her eyes really were the color of butterscotch; imagine Rain MacCallum noticing. How well had he known that girl out west, she wondered. She was turning away when she heard tires on the gravel. Diners? It was ten minutes to twelve. She blew a kiss at Monsieur Thierry taped to the mirror and dashed downstairs.

It was the dairy man, good as his word, with the whipping cream. Across the road, the men were laying down their tools. Off to Le Casse-Croûte, she supposed. With luck, they'd take an hour; the silence was heavenly. She detoured through the office and put on a Vivaldi cassette. Monsieur Thierry on the bulletin board frowned as the violins flooded the room with Italian sunshine.

In the kitchen the soup was hot, the quiches transferred to the warming oven, the coffee percolating in the coffee maker. Madame Hebert, her arms neatly folded across her chest, leaned against the sink.

"It does not appear to be a stampede."

"No." It was four minutes past twelve on the daisy clock.

"In a small town, people take their time to try something new. They are careful."

"Of course. And it's early yet for tourists. The season really only starts at the end of June."

She had taken that into consideration when she planned her opening date—time to iron out the wrinkles. Still, it would be nice to have some diners to practice on. She was in the office, copying the milk bill into accounts payable, when work boots clumped across the porch and male voices sounded in the foyer.

Halfway across the dining room, she stopped short. Rain grinned down at her, the breadth of his shoulders filling the doorway. "Since breakfast didn't work out, I thought we'd try for lunch."

She mumbled a reply; her voice seemed to have left her.

"Unless, of course, you're full up?"

She intercepted the glance he sent around the empty tables. "If you've come to gloat . . ."

"Not at all. It's not obligatory is it?"

She picked up menus at the reception desk and led the way. "Inside? Or out in the sun room?" she asked stiffly.

"The sun room, maybe?" he asked his companions. He winked at Joy. "Didn't have time to put on jackets and ties."

She could see they had made an effort to clean up. Hands washed, hair smoothed back. Still, their jeans sported streaks of drying concrete. They chose a shaded table and sat down. It had obviously been Rain's idea to come; the other two looked ill at ease and glanced at the hanging begonias as though expecting them to crash down any second. She handed out the menus. She wasn't feeling all that self-assured herself. Her first diners, and one of them had to be Rain MacCallum. The way his bright roving eyes were taking things in, she couldn't quite believe he hadn't come to assess his chances at the cottage. She told them the special, adding, "No *patates frites*. But if you prefer, I could make sandwiches." She hesitated, not wanting to sound patronizing.

"Quiche sounds fine. Especially when the boss is footing the bill. Right, men?"

Whatever their usual fare, all three plainly enjoyed what she put before them. Bursts of laughter brought the empty café to life. Rain had a good rapport with his men, she noticed, half listening as she added up the bill at the sideboard. His resonant baritone returned their banter in the easy joual that was the dialect of Québec. He was the last to leave, pocketing the remaining hermit.

He took her hand in his firm brown one and raised it to his lips. "My compliments to the chef. Fine food, charmingly served. We didn't lower the tone too much?''

She recovered her hand and shook her head, oddly moved. "Without you, the ButterCup's grand opening wouldn't have *had* a tone."

"People will come. You'll see." He placed a finger lightly under her chin and looked into her eyes. "Trust me."

Bemused, she carried the coffee cups into the kitchen. An odd thing for him to say; she didn't think she liked the sound of it. As though her success or failure lay in his hands. She wished she didn't still feel the imprint of his finger on her skin. "Well," she observed briskly, with an eye on the clock, "that seems to be it for lunch. We might as well sit down and treat ourselves to left-over quiche before we start on the vegetables for tonight."

Madame Hebert gave a wintry smile, her first, and put the kettle on for tea. She wasn't much for conversation, but she was an excellent worker and they got through the dinner preparations with plenty of time for Joy to shower and change for the evening shift. She trailed up the stairs with JS at her heels. What if no one showed up for dinner? What if Rain felt sorry for her and brought his crew over a second time? The embarrassment would be hard to swallow. She put on her pleated black skirt and high-necked white blouse with the elegant tucking, and felt somewhat cheered. Hovering in the back of her mind was a silly hope that Rain might see her in it.

She was adding seed-pearl earrings, when the late-afternoon sun turned everything on her dresser to crystal and gold. She walked to the open balcony door.

Amazing, the havoc three men could wreak on a beach in a day. The skeleton of the wharf lay clearly defined below, bulkier than she'd expected. But then, so was the boat. Nothing seemed to turn out as she expected, when Rain MacCallum was involved. He'd stripped to his jeans and was wading in the water. His muscular torso looked dipped in bronze. Just watching him made a funny tremor run through her stomach. Why couldn't she have met him at Lloyd & Upshaw's, decently clothed in a three-piece suit and doing nine-to-five work that wasn't a threat to her own? A smile escaped her at the thought. Men like Rain didn't work in windowless cubicles on twenty-first floors, any more than men like Brian built wharves and disfigured the landscape.

JS let out a plaintive meow and she scooped him up for a hug. It seemed ages since Grabber had bounded onto the scene, bringing unexpected complications into their lives. "A veal bird for dinner tonight," she promised him.

The six o'clock news had just come on when a fleet of cars turned into the lot, led by Clémence's sporty red two-seater. Her silver-blond hair was brushed into fashionable disarray, her size eight figure whip-slender in two-piece *café-au-lait* lace. She kissed Joy on both cheeks and held her at arm's length. "*Ma petite*, how charmingly *jeune-fille* you look!" A wave of Madame Rochas perfume swirled in her wake as she took in the water-color prints in the dining room, the spring nosegays on the yellow linen tablecloths. "What a marvelous job you have done! A shame the MacCallum boy could not have waited a few days with his wharf. Although, now that I see him out there, I think maybe he is worth it, *non?* You did not tell me he is so hand-some."

"Didn't I?" said Joy and Clémence gave her a keen look. More and more people were crowding into the foyer, and she leaned closer. "Some of your best wine, perhaps? I have persuaded several of my friends to join me for supper. As I told the mayor, it is not every day Lac Désir acquires a chic new eating spot to draw the tourists."

Joy beamed and reached for the menus. "Clémence, you're an angel."

She had to speak up to make herself heard. The talk and laughter among the handsomely dressed crowd was exuberant. Just as well; Vivaldi alone would never have been enough to mask the pounding and hammering across the road. It was warm for June and the windows were open; several times she found herself apologizing. When the sunset arrived, on cue and spectacular as a Tom Thomson painting, she held her breath. Surely now they'd stop work. Instead, Rain rigged up his portable light and filled the night with the hissing roar of a blowtorch. If she hadn't been run off her feet, with every table taken, she'd have marched over and grabbed the torch out of his hands herself.

"Do not worry yourself," murmured Clémence, as Joy slid a dish of maple charlotte, resplendent with whipped cream, in front of her. "Noise never bothers a Québecois. And with food like this, why should it?"

She let out her breath; Clémence was right, of course. But her irritation flared anew when, many cups of Irish coffee later, the first car to leave the lot was struck on the fender by a truck pulling abruptly away from the opposite shoulder. Rain himself came over to inspect the damage.

"No problem. Insurance will cover it."

Joy was furious and refused to meet his placating look.

"Peace offering," he declared, as the last taillight dwindled down the road. "I'm a great hand with dishes. Bet you've got a kitchenful after that crowd."

"The ButterCup has a dishwasher." She turned on him, skirt swirling about her knees, her voice edged with suppressed tears. "That was the mayor's Cadillac! Haven't you done enough damage for one night?"

He shrugged, palms upward. He had blisters large as quarters. "It was his own fault. Probably had one too many with dinner. What did you cook?"

"Veal birds. With mushrooms and wild rice. If people even noticed over the racket you were making."

He grinned. His hair was matted, his face smudged and lined with fatigue. "Any left over?"

"No!" she shouted and ran up the steps and slammed the front door.

Madame Hebert glanced at her red face but kept on loading the dishwasher.

"It's late. I'll finish up tonight." Joy stuffed the remaining veal birds into a plastic container. "Here, take these for your family." Madame Hebert was a widow with three children still at home and a grandchild. If anyone merited leftover veal birds it was the Heberts and not Rain MacCallum.

It was close to midnight by the time she switched on the little amber-shaded lamp on her nightstand. JS, already curled up at the foot of the bed, blinked reproachfully. She couldn't believe anyone could feel so tired and still be alive. It took all her strength to kick off her black pumps and totter into the bathroom to brush her teeth.

Monsieur Thierry's disapproving visage behind the glass door of the medicine cabinet revived her slightly. Even he would have to be impressed by tonight's cash intake. She daubed a brash toothpaste mustache over his prim lips. Then, stretched out in a cool cotton nightgown, with JS rumbling companionably and moonlight spilling between the slats of the blind, she gave herself up to sleep. But her eyes refused to close.

The quiet made her uneasy; she wasn't used to it. She slipped out of bed and poked the slats apart. The portable light had been turned off. The trucks were gone, all except Rain's. The embers of a wood fire glowed in the sand. A flattened white shape sprawled nearby could be Grabber; maybe that bumpy log in the shadows was Rain, rolled up in a sleeping bag. She wondered what it was like, sleeping in the sand. He'd looked exhausted. Had he eaten anything? The moon unfurled a broad silver ribbon across the bay and over the metal roof of the Lac Désir church. She'd been awfully rude to him. She'd had every reason, of course; give some men an inch and they took a yard. It made no sense, but she wished she were down there. She trailed back to bed.

If she didn't fall asleep soon, it would be too late. He'd be up with his chainsaw or his blowtorch or whatever he had planned for today. She pulled the duvet over her head. Another day at this rate, and the wharf would be finished. If she lasted that long.

The next day was Friday and an almost total repeat of the previous day. But when she opened her eyes on Saturday, silence reigned. She could hear the robins reaffirming their claim to the lilacs, and the gentle lapping of waves on the beach. Disbelieving, she stared at the clock. It read 8:20. She swung her legs over the side of the bed and for a moment she wondered if she were

dreaming. Outside where sky should be, floated a giant
tarpaper banner. Scrawled across it in white paint was
the message

> Good morning sleepyhead
> sorry about the last 2 nights
> gone today—Enjoy!

She started to giggle helplessly. You had to give him
marks for ingenuity. He had fastened the tarpaper to the
top of his light pole and thrust it into her marigold bed.
There was no sign of him, or the truck. The cement
mixer stood abandoned amid a drift of empty cement
bags. But the wharf looked impressive in the morning
sun. It appeared to be finished, except for stain or paint,
or whatever he was going to put on it. Maybe he'd gone
into town to buy some, or maybe he was checking on
the houseboat. She certainly was not going to miss him.

The start of the weekend and the weather was glo-
rious; tourists would be swarming all over the Laurentians. If they'd read her ad in the Montréal papers,
they'd include a stop at Lac Désir. She reached for
shorts. She'd have to get rid of that banner, preferably
before Madame Hebert arrived, or the dairy truck or
some boy on a bicycle from town. She hated to think
what interpretation they'd put on Rain's message.

Things started off well, with two elderly couples from
Ontario stopping for coffee in the sun room and finding the peonies and the lake and the attentions of JS so
delightful, they stayed for a leisurely lunch. But Saturday night failed to produce the swinging crowd Joy had
hoped for. Two girls in turquoise eyeshadow settled
grudgingly for Croque Monsieur when they couldn't get
hamburgers. Twenty minutes later they left and that was

it. At seven-thirty, she gave Madame Hebert the rest of the evening off.

"Maybe if you had a bar. A video screen," offered Madame Hebert.

"Heaven forbid," said Joy, packing untouched Coq au Vin for the little Heberts.

It hadn't been a day to set Monsieur Thierry's mind at ease about the mortgage. Nor Brian's, about women in business on their own. Restlessly, she eyed the carnations and wondered whether they'd faded sufficiently for her to throw them out. *He knows I've opened. He could have called. Asked how it's going.* On balance, though, she was relieved he hadn't. It was surprising how little she missed him. If she missed anything, it was the hurly-burly across the road—with Rain in its midst. The thought alarmed her. Maybe what she needed was a cold swim, to shock some sense back into her.

The beach had certainly changed in the short week since she'd walked here last, breathing in its beauty and tranquility. Trudging across the sand through a welter of planks, ruts and spilled nails was enough to start her resentment flowing again. The mess was only temporary; still, it didn't bode well for Rain's skill at housekeeping once the boat arrived. She tried not to think about it. She dropped her towel on a log and waded slowly into the water, letting the evening work its magic. The sun was sinking behind her favorite mountain. Towering cloud castles flamed in the west, reflected by the glass-smooth water of the lake. It took a moment for the rumble of a vehicle to penetrate her consciousness.

Even before it slowed, she recognized Rain's truck. Like a fool, she'd put on her oldest bathing suit, a green print bikini that would have looked scanty on someone ten pounds lighter. She ducked to meet the water and swam away in a panic, just as the cab door slammed behind her.

"Joy! Joy Lowry!" he shouted. He sounded angry.

Let him. The water flowed over her shoulders like crimson silk and she felt a surge of exhilaration. He shouted again and lazily she turned. "What?"

He stood with hands on slim blue-jeaned hips, square-toed work boots planted aggressively at the water's edge, while Grabber galloped back and forth, barking. "Come back! You shouldn't be out there!"

"Why not? The cottage has access to the lake. It's in the deed."

"To hell with the deed! I'm not talking about access. It's dangerous. Only an idiot would swim on a building site in the dark."

"Dark?" She flung back her head and gave an exuberant laugh. Even the air glowed with fiery light.

"You know damn well what I mean. Ever heard of deadheads? Some of the logs got away from us and submerged. You'll scrape yourself open before you even see them."

A made-up story if she'd ever heard one. A ploy to keep her off the beach, maybe even to make the cottage seem less worth having. She wouldn't put it past him.

"Are you deaf, woman? Or just stupid? Get back here!"

Overbearing male. Just like Brian when he couldn't get what he wanted. She turned on her stomach and pulled away. "When I'm ready. Not before."

He swore. She looked back in astonishment. She'd never made a man so angry he swore. He was hopping on one foot, tugging at a boot. In one fluid motion he peeled off his T-shirt and flung it on the sand. Long splashing strides brought him into the water. She gave an involuntary shriek and swam for all she was worth.

CHAPTER THREE

TERRIFYINGLY SOONER than she'd have thought possible, his heavy hand closed over her shoulder. She jerked sideways, swallowing water and sputtering.

"Take it easy." The hand stayed where it was, supporting her. "What did you think? That I was planning to drown you?"

Water spiked his hair and beard, even his eyelashes. She glared back at him. The feel of his hand on her wet skin was unbelievably intimate. With powerful strokes he began to draw her through the smoldering water. "Look!"

Looming just below the surface, she made out the slanting jagged end of a log. Her stomach contracted with a tingling sensation.

"Oh."

"The other end is lodged in the mud. Tomorrow I'll attach a cable. Haul it out with the truck." He was still angry. "If I'd known you were going to take it into your silly head to go swimming..."

"How was I to know you were making a minefield of the place?" she flared. But the colors were dying overhead and the water felt colder than it had. She was aware of a new, unreasoning fear of the depths below. Hard as she'd been trying to escape earlier, she now kept close to him.

"It's all right," he said, more quietly. "We're past them now." Her feet touched bottom. He kept his hand on her elbow as they waded ashore. She was shivering; a hint of shock, she supposed. Grabber's wet nose on her hand was sympathetic. Rain scooped up her towel and draped it over her shoulders. Big gentle hands turned her to face him, then began vigorously rubbing her back.

"Really, you don't..." Her voice trailed away. The shivering subsided and a sensation of warmth and well-being radiated from her spine. She stood like a child and simply let it happen.

Bending his wet brown head, he dropped a kiss on her lips. It was over too quickly for her to protest. "How does cocoa by the campfire sound to you?" he asked.

She laughed, her lips tingling. She thought of the embers on the beach the other night. "You must have been a Boy Scout. Lifesaving. Campfire cooking."

"Comes of growing up in the country. I bet—" he pulled the T-shirt over his head and emerged, grinning "—you'd do the same for me if you found me wandering on the train tracks in Montréal." His head was plastered with ringlets almost as curly as her own.

"If I did, I hope you'd be more cooperative than I was. Have I said thank you yet? It was kind of you to be concerned. Even though you yelled at me."

He snorted, and leaned some odds and ends of lumber together in the scooped-out hollow that held the other night's ashes. "Not just kind. Smart, too. If anything had happened, you could have slapped me with a lawsuit."

"I'll keep that in mind. In case you have another project up your sleeve."

He lit a match. She sat on the log with her towel wrapped around her. The flame licked at a shaving, flickered, then took hold. Grabber sighed and flopped down on the other side. In the sky, the mauve banners were fading. "I know you're not exactly thrilled with what I'm doing on the beach," he said.

"Well. I liked it the way it was. Natural and unspoiled."

He nodded, then bent over the toolbox in the back of the truck and came up with a dented saucepan, a tin of cocoa and a carton of milk. "I will say this. The houseboat's one hundred percent natural. Wood construction throughout. Hand-carved shutters. Cedar shingles on the roof."

She had seen outhouses on the outskirts of Lac Désir that fitted his description. "Is that where you were today? With the houseboat?"

"Arranging for transportation, actually. Getting it to the lake is going to be tougher than I thought."

She waited.

"It's a little—well, big." He had the grace to look apologetic.

"Really?"

"Aren't you curious?"

"About the houseboat?" She didn't tell him she'd been nursing a forlorn hope the railway might have mislaid it on a siding. Shipped it on to Halifax, possibly.

He looked at her sidelong, the whites of his eyes gleaming in the firelight. "You look so cute when you're trying to be tactful."

"It's not a joke, for heaven's sake. What you do with the beach affects my livelihood. My future."

"Mine, too," he said reasonably. He filled tin mugs and handed her one. "Careful. It's hot. What do you want me to do? Sail the rivers of Canada for the rest of my life?"

"Like the Flying Dutchman in the opera." She smiled at the image: Rain in a cloak, with a gold earring in one ear and the wind billowing the sails above his streaming hair.

"Wagner," he declared, "right?" and lowered himself next to her. He stretched out long blue-jeaned legs where the heat could get at them. "For a café proprietor, you know an awful lot about music."

"We always had music at home. My mother was a concert cellist. Catherine Lowry. She died in a plane crash when I was eight. Mostly I remember her now as a presence, lovely and shining..."

"And your father?" he asked quietly.

"I didn't see much of him after Mother died. He traveled a lot. Maybe drifted is a better word. My Aunt May raised me." She turned and saw her face reflected in his eyes, open and steady. "She's the one who taught me to love this place. Taught me how to cook, too."

They sat for a while, drinking their cocoa. It didn't seem necessary to talk; she liked that. His presence filled a void she had been carrying around with her a long time. He leaned forward and threw a piece of wood on the fire. Mischief tugged at his lips.

"So what's the verdict? Is Rain MacCallum doomed to ply the Fraser, or the St. Lawrence, or the Miramichi, until he finds a woman willing to sacrifice her life for love?"

An unaccustomed shyness stole over her. She looked into her mug. "Can't you just live in a normal house? Like a normal man?"

"You'd be surprised how normal I am," he said softly, and his shoulder touched hers. The warmth of it came as a shock through her towel. "It's just that somebody happens to be living in my house."

"That's not fair!" She drew herself up. "If you're so crazy about the cottage, why did you sell it? Couldn't you just have locked the door and left?"

"It was the only way I could make the money I needed to get my start. I always planned some day to come back and reclaim the place." He said it matter-of-factly, as though she were only a temporary roadblock.

"Over my dead body," she declared, startling herself.

His strong full lips were quirked at one corner with suppressed humor. "Damned if you don't look even cuter when you're trying to be rude."

"Don't patronize me!" she flashed. Her towel slipped with the jerk of her arm. Hastily she drew it up again. This was not the time to remind him of how little she was wearing.

"You're right, Miss Lowry. A man should know better in this day and age." He leaned back with an air of having lost interest, and she felt a perverse sense of letdown. He stretched muscular arms above his head and drew in a lungful of air.

"You can smell the lilac all the way down here. Did you know my grandfather planted that hedge?"

"You want me to feel guilty, Mr. MacCallum?"

"It's up to you." He shrugged. "It was a wedding present for my grandmother. The cottage was just a cabin in the bush then. No road. They had to cross the bay in a boat."

She thought of the young couple rowing home in the soft summer dusk. "They must have been very much in love."

The word love seemed to hang in the air. His hand brushed hers, stirring feelings she was working to subdue. "Warm enough now?" he asked.

She murmured a reply. The lights of Lac Désir shimmered in the water, gold and orange. The sound of dance music drifted across the lake, filling her with the strangest longing that was all mixed up with the presence of the man beside her.

"Good times over there tonight," he said lazily. "You closed up early for a Saturday, didn't you?"

She should have known better than to let her guard down, even for a minute. "I suppose that pleases you?"

"Why should it? Just because we're after the same thing?" He studied her. "Maybe we should cease hostilities and try a little cooperation."

"Maybe *you* should. I've got the cottage."

"And I've got the beach." His eyebrows shot up. "Impasse." He drained his mug, dropped it on the sand and slid his arm around her all in one swift motion. "You realize all the world's best solutions come about as a result of impasses?"

"The world's wars, too." She laughed breathlessly. His closeness made it difficult to think. Her heart was thumping like one of his machines. "Is this your idea of cooperation?"

"You have a better one?"

"Rain, please. Be serious for once, can't you?"

"I am." His eyes dropped to her lips with devastating effect. "You have no idea how serious."

"Oh..."

She wasn't sure how it happened, but all at once he was kissing her and she was letting him. The bristles of his mustache prickled silkily on her upper lip. His full soft lips pressed against her own with a sideways caressing motion that made her eyelids flutter shut and sent a sharp tremor arrowing down from the direction of her heart.

The pressure of his lips became more urgent, and helplessly her own began to part. A delicious warmth spread through her. His hands found their way under the towel to her shoulders. He drew her close and her upper body arched forward, encouraging him. She forgot about holding the towel closed and her hands crept up around the back of his neck. A little sigh escaped her as her fingers came in contact with the hair growing in soft whorls down to his nape. The tip of his tongue entered her mouth, probing delicately, withdrawing, entering more boldly until it touched her own, and again the tremor ran through her, like a hot wire that was infinitely more pleasure than pain. A smothered groan broke from Rain's throat and she realized he felt the same thing.

His hands moved, exploring in a slow circular motion her back and the bare tender flesh of her waist. They came to rest, warm and heavy, on the ripe curves of her hips. The kiss ended then, and they drew back to stare at each other's faces. She couldn't remember now why she had been afraid of what she saw in his eyes. She watched them slip from her face, over her neck, down to her breasts. Firelight threw the curves, swelling out of their scanty cloth covering, into golden relief and made a mysterious shadowy valley of the space between.

"Joy... Joy," he breathed, "you're beautiful."

She gave him a tremulous smile. Her hand groped in the sand for her towel. "I really should be going."

"Why?"

He sat relaxed, with his head thrown back, not moving, drinking her in. A breath of air came up from the lake, cooling her cheeks. It ruffled the coppery hair falling over his forehead, and she stood up to keep from reaching over and touching it, touching his face. She didn't bother with the towel. He had called her beautiful. She couldn't tell him that he was the reason she had to go. He was dangerous; with one kiss he had aroused responses in her she wasn't sure she could control: something Brian, for all his knowledge of when to send flowers and how to tip the maître d'hôtel for a private table, had never come close to doing. It made her afraid of what might happen next.

She kept her tone light. "Morning has a habit of arriving early around here."

A stick of wood collapsed in a shower of ash and some of the glow went out of his face. He got to his feet. "You have a point. Grabber and I will see you across the road." He signaled the dog and tucked her hand under his arm. "All those lilac bushes. Who knows what evil lurks..."

Joy laughed and tried not to feel disappointed that he had given up so easily. She marvelled at the way he walked across the gravel road in his bare feet without flinching. The moon was climbing the cottage roof. In the shadow of the porch, he cupped his hands about her face and kissed her again, lingeringly, as though he liked the taste of her. "I almost forgot to tell you." His eyes were musing and dark, mysterious as the pine forest on the hill.

"What?"

"I heard in Lac Désir today, the old Quenneville place is for sale."

She stared at him.

"Big mahogany-paneled dining room. I happen to know the kitchen's been renovated. Right on rue Principale. Business would be good there."

"How could you?" she exclaimed hoarsely. "How *could* you! When we—when you've just—"

"What's the matter with you? All I said was—"

"I heard what you said!" She felt as though her blood had turned to ice. "Whatever you think you're offering in return, Mr. MacCallum, it's not enough to make me give up the cottage. No matter how you dress it up. So in future, I suggest you spare us both the waste of time."

She thrust blindly past him, slipped through the door and slammed it in his face.

CHAPTER FOUR

RAIN WAS OUTSIDE all day Sunday, staining the wharf a weathered gray in the brilliant sunshine. She didn't set foot out the front door once. Of course he was going to try to apologize, bluff his way out of what he'd let slip with some explanation or other. And she didn't want to hear it. But she couldn't resist glancing out at him now and then . . . He peeled off his T-shirt and whistled old Beatles tunes with Grabber drowsing beside him. There was a regatta being held at Lac Désir and the white sails tacking over the blue water made a handsome back-drop. At one o'clock he rattled off in the truck and returned with a carton from Le Casse-Croûte, which he proceeded to share with Grabber while the two of them stretched out on the sand and watched the race.

"If he wants to eat alone, let him," she thought, pausing by the bow window with a tray of freshly washed and filled sugar bowls. Diners were few. Her eyelids were shadowed from lack of sleep, and even her upper lip had a subdued look to it. A man who built houseboats for a living—she should have known better. It was probably all a game to him: life, the boat, the wharf, the kiss. She plunked down the tray and marched around the room putting the sugar bowls back. Especially the kiss. That was a game with a prize at the end, if he played it right.

Critically, she straightened a wineglass and plucked a wilted buttercup out of a nosegay of daisies and buttercups.

It was ironic. She used to wonder why her mind began constructing lasagne or mocha torte whenever Brian, or one or two of the others she'd gone out with in the past, had tried to kiss her. Last night, she'd discovered she had simply been waiting for a man like Rain MacCallum to kiss her. And now it turned out that all he wanted was the cottage. She thought about it again Sunday night before she fell asleep. That, and the way his eyes had looked when he told her she was beautiful.

On Monday morning, she was shaving chocolate curls onto the luncheon mousse and feeling inexplicably restless, when car horns blared on the road.

"Now what?" she snapped, causing JS to drop a planned investigation of the cheese tarts cooling on the table. She switched off the radio—some pianist crashing chords—as bicycle bells and barking dogs joined the honking. Half a dozen cars, by the sound of it, swooped into her parking lot. A spur-of-the-moment wedding party? She had made only a dozen cheese tarts but there were all those stuffed green peppers left from yesterday. She checked the little mirror fastened to the door jamb for chocolate on her face and hurried to unlock the front door.

If it was a wedding party, half the town had been invited. Cars, trucks and vans were pulling up everywhere, spilling out people. School must have let out, too. Children were streaming along the road all the way back to the bend, interspersed with mothers pushing strollers. Like a kaleidoscope, the crowd shifted, revealing Rain directing traffic. At the sight of his long brown legs in cutoff jeans a melting sensation threatened to engulf her. She caught herself immediately.

The houseboat! It dawned on her. "A floating circus," Clémence had called it, and every circus came with a parade. The girls from the Supermarché were lining up on her lawn. She thought she saw the mayor's Cadillac stuck in the sand. A bus backed over her marigolds and she winced. Maybe if she went and stood on the steps, people wouldn't be so reckless. Rain, his windblown brown head topping everybody else's, waved at her. She didn't look away fast enough, and he blew her an extravagant kiss. She stared up the road, feeling her cheeks turn crimson. A Sûreté Québec constable rumbled up on a motorcycle and started clearing a path to the beach. People cheered.

The masts appeared first, gliding over the treetops, followed by a rusty stovepipe. Then the blunt-nosed prow emerged from behind the trees and spread across the entire width of the road behind a chugging diesel tractor. Joy felt disbelief, then anger. It wasn't a boat, it was a barge. Ladders connected a rambling superstructure of decks and cabins with rooftops of varying levels. No two windows were the same size. A green-and-white awning shaded the afterdeck, and giant letters spelled out La Grosse Grenouille on the weathered stern. Just before the crowd surged onto the beach behind it, she caught a glimpse of Rain's face, transfigured like a small boy's at Christmas. She sat down on the step, her knees weak. The Bullfrog, indeed; what else could he call it?

Clémence emerged from the crowd, makeup flawless, totally chic in a belted silk shirt over white slacks. "Well, does it look as I said?"

"Worse," answered Joy disconsolately. It certainly was green, and talk about blocking the view! Her diners would think they were tuned in to a houseboat channel on television. She didn't have the strength to get up.

"Where is Madame Hebert? In the kitchen?"

"No. I told her to take a couple of days off."

"*Mon dieu!* How will you manage with all this crowd?"

"They're not coming here. Are they?"

"Why not?" She raised a slim arm to consult a wafer-thin gold watch. "It is noon. A holiday event. What better place for front-row seats?"

Joy scrambled to her feet. Already two couples were strolling up the path; a family with children was pointing at the sun room. Halfway to the kitchen she turned back. "Clémence, could you phone Madame Hebert for me? See how fast she can get here?"

"Better still, I will look in the crowd. I saw her grandson a moment ago. Doubtless she brought him herself."

"You're a lifesaver, Clémence! I'll get the peppers on. Let's hope JS hasn't eaten the mousse."

He hadn't. Thank heavens, she was still in business. From now on, she'd have to remember she was running a restaurant. She thrust the mousse into the refrigerator and snatched out the peppers. Voices sounded in the foyer: Clémence, along with the couples. "She is on her way. She was already looking for her daughter to take the boy home. Shall I show these ladies and gentlemen to a table?"

"Please! Menus on the desk. I'll be right with them."

She managed. Panic was confined to the kitchen. Madame Hebert walked in steely eyed, reached for her apron and turned out salads in six minutes flat. Clémence, high heels clicking graciously, stayed on for an hour as hostess. Joy was pouring coffee in the sun room when a rumble of thunder swelled up from the beach. She looked just in time to see the houseboat rolling grandly down a log ramp into the water. A straining army of volunteers pushed and tugged. Rain had shed his boots as well as his shirt. His taut brown body glistened in the sun as he swung up a ladder and attached a folded cloth to the rear mast. As he stood with head flung back and shoulders squared, watching the breeze unfurl the blue-and-white fleur-de-lis of Québec, Joy caught his young man's mood of pride and fierce elation and smiled with him. Insanely, she wanted to rush out on the beach and link arms and cheer with the crowd.

"Mademoiselle? Cream? Could we have some cream?" the customers at a nearby table asked, and she came back to earth with a jolt. The last thing Rain MacCallum needed was encouraging.

By the time the last diner left, they had served eight tables twice over. Madame Hebert made sandwiches and a pot of tea. Joy locked the cash away and grinned smugly at Monsieur Thierry.

"Sorry there was only cheese left," she said, sitting down. She wondered if Rain had anything to eat in his galley; maybe he'd gone to Le Casse-Croûte with the others. She propped her tired feet up and noticed her jeans. "I never changed," she said, surprised.

Madame Hebert chewed without comment. "Have you decided on a vegetable to go with the Porc Brochettes tonight?"

"Peas from the garden, I think. I'll have to drive into town for more bread. Although I doubt we'll need it.

The excitement's over and we won't get another crowd like this one.''

She was wrong. They had three sittings that evening, and at ten the next morning she was putting up extra tables in the sun room so people could enjoy the view with coffee and hurriedly baked muffins. For the evening shift, Madame Hebert's fifteen-year-old daughter was pressed into service to fill water glasses and bread baskets, and stack the dishwasher. When Rain showed up after dark asking for Joy, she sent the girl to tell him she was busy. He had certainly taken his time to come around—three days since he'd spoiled everything by mentioning the Quenneville place. He needn't think she was waiting with bated breath for him to talk his way out of it.

"Where did they all come from?" she sighed, exhausted, as she saw the Heberts off long after eleven. There wasn't a crumb left to put in a shopping bag.

The older woman shrugged. "It is the only houseboat in the Laurentians. So far."

"Lucky for the Laurentians," she thought, sliding the balcony door shut in spite of the warm night. It sounded like a party down there. Cars coming and going, music blaring, people on the decks. Maybe he was already making sales. Lamps glowed in the houseboat windows, casting wavery gold reflections on the water. Joy thought of the funny lurch her heart had given at the sight of him, brown and substantial, across the crowded dining room. She drew the blinds tight. A long time later she heard him laughing in that way he had, right up from his boot soles, and she dragged the pillow over her head.

She pulled herself out of bed at dawn. She had no choice if she wanted to keep up with the baking. Yawning, she saw that Rain had awakened first. The stove-pipe, newly shined, was already sending up a plume of smoke. Stretched between two masts was a scroll of tarpaper reading, "Joy, come for breakfast. We have to talk."

A little stab went through her before she turned to reach for clean cotton slacks. How simple it would be just to follow her inclination! Not that she would, if she knew what was good for her—and for the café.

All the same, a sigh of regret escaped her as she searched the drawer for a top. She told herself it would have been interesting to see the inside of the house-boat. What had he planned to offer her? Fruit and scrambled eggs? Maple syrup on French toast? A bowl of corn flakes? She had no idea what Rain ate for breakfast; somehow it made a hole in the day, not knowing, and that annoyed her too. She held up a dove-gray polo pullover, to match the mood of the morning. For the first time in a week the sky was overcast.

The radio predicted rain; Madame Hebert felt it in her bunions. The weather seemed to have an effect on the number of diners, too. By one-thirty they had the kitchen shipshape and the Closed sign out and Joy was pushing the lawnmower across the front lawn. Hammering sounded from inside the boat. Hands on hips, she regarded her lawn. Tire tracks in the grass, half the marigolds flat, litter like confetti dotting the green. She was on her knees, tenderly taping a marigold stem, when a pair of size-twelve Adidas materialized. Rain—she hadn't realized the hammering had stopped. At least he was fully clothed today. He was wearing a moss-colored sweatshirt that proclaimed Houseboaters Do It In Waves. She averted her eyes and waited for him to make the first move.

"What's this? First aid for flowers? I didn't know restaurateurs had to be so multitalented."

"They do when they live opposite sideshow attractions. Look at this—this mess!"

"Oho!" He paused. "Is that why I've been getting the cold shoulder? Having my invitations ignored?"

"No."

"Just no?"

"You really want me to tell you? You haven't figured it out for yourself yet?"

"Try me."

His eyes when she met them head-on dazzled like sun on the water. It was three days since she had looked into those eyes and seen how deep and warm they were.

"All right." She sat back on her heels, pushed a dirt-smudged hand through the curls on her forehead. "All right, maybe I will. You think you're pretty macho, don't you? Stop grinning like that or I won't go on. You think all you have to do is flaunt your sex appeal. Tell a woman she's beautiful. Give her—" her voice sank in spite of herself "—one of your kisses and she'll do anything for you."

His brow rose quizzically. "Anything? I wasn't aware I'd asked."

Her cheeks flamed. "I don't mean . . . that. Whatever you're thinking. I'm talking about the cottage. That's what you're after, isn't it? Triumphant houseboat impresario returns to reclaim boyhood home. By any means available."

Rain gave a whoop of laughter that sent a robin scolding to the porch roof. She threw a punch at his knees, which he nimbly sidestepped.

"You haven't even got the decency to deny it!"

"Would it help?"

Her shoulders sagged. "No. You made it humiliatingly plain. One minute I'm in your arms. The next you're talking about a house for sale on rue Principale."

He shrugged. "I admit the timing was unfortunate."

"Only the timing?" She felt the helpless anger rising in her all over again. "Do you always use people like that?"

His face was suddenly cold sober, his tone flat. "It didn't enter your head—before you slammed the door in my face—that it might make good business sense to know of another location? In case you don't make a go of it here?"

She was stubbornly silent; it sounded like a threat to her. The crinkles crept back to the corners of his eyes. "Would you rather I'd wanted to go to bed with you?"

Her chest tightened alarmingly. "I . . . I could have understood that. Even . . . excused it."

"I'll keep that in mind for the next time."

She stood up, pocketed the tape and brushed off her knees. "If there is a next time."

"And this time? Am I forgiven?"

She looked at him. She had the feeling she'd missed something. As though she'd scored a point, but he was leading in the game. Her gaze shifted to the Bullfrog, hulking greenly in the reeds. "On probation, maybe. Seeing we're going to be stuck with each other as neighbors."

"You make it sound like I'm a union organizer for kitchen staff." When she smiled in spite of herself, he added, "Admit it. The spin-off hasn't been all bad."

"No. Apart from the marigolds and Madam Hebert's feet." Honesty got the better of her. "Frankly, the houseboat's made all the difference. I was able to make my mortgage payment yesterday and Monsieur Thierry actually smiled at me. Not that I expect you to see that as a positive result.''

He grinned. ''You don't give up, do you?''

''I can't afford to.''

His teeth gleamed like oyster shell under the brown mustache. ''Two of a kind. Truce?'' He held out his hand.

It felt disturbingly familiar.

''Will you come over and see her? 'In Xanadu did Kubla Khan a stately pleasure dome decree.''' The lines from Coleridge took on a seductive quality as he waited for her yes. He was still holding her hand.

''Now?''

''Best time.'' He glanced up and caught a raindrop on his beard. ''It's starting to drizzle.''

Protest died in her throat. For the life of her, she couldn't remember any of her reasons for avoiding him. Maybe it was the effect of his hand, securely folded around her own. There was something so trustworthy about the feel of male calluses.

CHAPTER FIVE

SHE LENGTHENED HER STRIDE to match his, unnervingly aware of the lean action of his hips next to hers. The beach was a shambles; she was shocked, seeing it up close.

"I can't keep them off it," he said ruefully. "People take pictures, bring kids, leave garbage. Worse still, they pick up things they have no right to. Souvenirs, they call them. Like my best drill, which disappeared yesterday. If it weren't for Grabber, they'd be all over the boat as well."

She took a deep breath. "Maybe if you cleaned up around here, you'd reduce temptation. This place is an eyesore from the café."

"Oh? Half the sightseers come from the café. They stroll down here working off their quiches and *coupes maisons*, blithely ignoring my Trespassers Will Be Prosecuted sign. Maybe you could point it out to them? Along with the special of the day?"

"As if they could miss it! Your sign has disfigured my birch tree—if the nails haven't already killed it. Anyway, stop changing the subject. I'm talking about these." She gestured angrily at a tumbled pile of sawed-off planks. "Those empty drums. The old rubber tires over there. Lac Désir has a dump, you know."

"Hey, wait a minute!" His hand on her arm swung her around to face him. "It's my beach, remember? I need this stuff for the boat. Repairs, renovations—it's an ongoing project."

She groaned inwardly. "*If* you don't mind," she said, removing his hand with none-too-steady fingers. "Then store it somewhere. What did you do on the Fraser?"

"I wintered at a marina. Rented a shed." He spread eloquent hands. "You see my problem."

But all she could see were his eyes, hypnotic and absorbing. "There's nothing I can do about it," she said weakly.

"Maybe there is. You've got the garage."

"With my Honda in it, yes."

"Which means it's half empty. I'll rent that half from you. Storage space."

"You mean for money? With a lease?" She made what she hoped was a landlady's face. "Renewable on a one-month basis?"

"Sure, why not? For both our protection." His eyes danced and she looked hastily away. "I'll think about it," she muttered. It would mean he could come and go on her property at will. She had an awful feeling she'd let him paint her into a corner. Why was it she couldn't say a simple 'no' to this man?

On the gangplank, she stopped short. "You've hung flower boxes on the railings." He'd planted them, too, with red-and-white Cherry Pie petunias. "And those little log birdhouses! Did you make them?"

"Long winter nights. Unmarried man has to keep busy," he said. Grabber came to meet them and he stooped to fondle the dog's ears. She could tell Rain was pleased.

Life preservers hung between the flower boxes. More green-and-white awning canopied the windows. *"Gai et charmant,"* Clémence had said. Evidently that—and not the mess on the beach—was what the diners saw when they flocked to ringside seats at the ButterCup. Maybe she'd been too prejudiced to notice.

"Mind the step." Rain sprang to the deck and turned to lift her down. For an instant she was aware of the close hard warmth of him and the way he smelled of clean shirts and wood shavings and some indefinable male essence.

"Mmm. Soft," he said, his hands buried in the pullover bunched at her waist. He held her a little apart so he could look at her.

"I've waited a long time to get you on board. I wanted you to be the first, remember? You're not, but you're here. So let's not spoil it by arguing anymore. About the cottage, or the beach, or who owns what. The diners, the noise, the dog, the cat. Nothing. Agreed?"

She swallowed. "I'm not arguing. If you—"

He pressed a finger to her lips and shook his head. "Nothing. For the next hour, you're a guest in my home. Agreed?"

She nodded with a detachment she didn't feel. His hands slid reluctantly from her waist, brushing her hips as they did, and she moved to the Dutch door standing half-open, revealing a shadowed interior. Her heart was racing, and that was the last thing she wanted him to know. In spite of all the warnings she'd had, his effect on her was proving to be just as difficult to control as it had been that night on the beach. If she had any sense, she'd turn right around and leave. A fine fool she'd look then. She could just see the mocking laughter in his eyes. She was uncharacteristically quiet as he showed her around.

"Aren't you going to tell me what you think?" he urged.

"I'm impressed. I had no idea it was so attractive."

Or so spacious. He had left most of the downstairs as one big room. West-coast cedar lent the walls a warm glow. The furnishings were masculine: big, comfortable chairs and a sofa piled with cushions covered in a sturdy blue-and-white sailcloth print. Floor-to-ceiling bookshelves flanked a glass-doored cast iron stove. A vivid splash of oranges and blues over the built-in bar turned out to be an abstract oil of a Vancouver regatta. She wondered about the wide array of bottles.

He winked. "They're part of the sales pitch. Actually, the houseboat sells itself. All you need is to get people on board for a few hours." He folded back cedar panels that opened the whole side of the room to the rear deck. Wicker chairs stood comfortably grouped around small tables under the shelter of the awning. There had to be half a dozen tables and nearly four times as many chairs. A feeling of uneasiness grew inside her, not relieved by the sight of a commercial-sized gas grill protruding from under a tarpaulin in the corner. Was there something he wasn't telling her? She noticed other things: the fact that he had rigged up loudspeakers to his stereo system and put candles in hurricane glasses on all the tables.

"Night is the best time," he was saying. "There's something magical about nights on the water."

"Like last night? And the night before?"

"Just people I used to know, dropping by. To a real party I invite the neighbors."

She smiled noncommittally and crossed to the rail. A light pearling drizzle dimpled the surface of the water, blurring the outline of the mountains. There was a fresh smell of reeds and water. He came and leaned beside her.

"Like a Japanese watercolor, isn't it? I never get tired of this view across the lake."

She looked at his Viking profile. "Somehow I hadn't thought of you as a man who knows about art. Or takes time for the view."

"Just because I wear work boots and drive a pickup?" He gave her a sidelong glance, eyes gleaming. "Stick around. I'm full of surprises."

The island halfway across the lake was a smudged pastel thumbprint. Their elbows touched; it could have been by accident. Almost in unison they turned and said, "You're getting wet."

They laughed. In the lounge they brushed the drops from their hair. His beard was full of diamonds. "Don't move," he ordered, then disappeared into the galley. Louvered shutters swung open and he reappeared, framed in a pass-through. "Coffee or Russian tea?"

"Russian tea?"

"Sure. Like this." He made tea in an earthenware pot and put it aside to steep. Then he set out glasses nested in wicker and spooned a generous dollop of raspberry preserve into each. She'd never seen a man so at home in a kitchen. She looked around her at the handsome fittings, the stainless steel sink and built-in modern appliances. Her glance lingered on a twelve-cup coffee maker; an awful lot of coffee for one person. Was it new? she wondered. Rain intercepted the glance, speaking before she could ask.

"Some long dry stretches on the Fraser—I always like to be prepared. Right now the boat's on a generator. But next week Hydro Québec's coming out to connect me to a power line. Might as well, since I'm going to be here for good." He poured the tea and looked straight at her as he handed her a fragrant, steaming glass. She felt such a rush of conflicting emotion that she turned and stared through a porthole at the cottage growing dark in the rain.

"There's a better view from upstairs."

"I—I should really be getting back. A party from Mont Tremblant has reservations and I'm making a strawberry flan. Besides, Madame Hebert—"

"Won't be back for another hour." He grinned wickedly. "What's the matter? Afraid of accepting an invitation to a man's bedroom?"

Alarm bells again. She stood very straight. "Of course not."

"Would it set your mind at ease if I told you I don't have a bed?"

"No bed?" She put down her glass, curiosity growing too big to handle, and followed him through the galley onto a pocket-sized deck with a freezer lining one wall and a ladder scaling the other. "There are inside stairs near the front door," he called back. "But this is closer." She was thankful for the overhanging roof as they climbed. A wind had sprung up, slanting the rain in fine silvery sheets that hit the water with a hissing sound. Timbers creaked with the movement of the boat. A wet swirling gust followed them onto the upstairs landing.

"Batten down the hatches," yelled Rain. "You take this side. I'll take that."

They ran from room to room, slamming windows and portholes, laughing. A cubbyhole under the eaves with a cluttered desk and a worn swivel chair was the double of her own office; instead of cookbooks, river charts and neat draftsman's sketches of houseboats lined the walls. On her way out, she noticed an invoice that had blown to the floor and picked it up.

"In here, Joy," called Rain. "Give me a hand?" She slipped the paper into her pocket and hurried to help.

He was trying to wind down a skylight, where a blind that had broken loose flapped like a mad sail through the opening. She tugged the blind back down, just as he lowered the skylight with a crash. They both stumbled backwards.

"Joy! Oh, Joy!" he said, laughing from his boot soles up and sliding his arms around her from behind. His strong brown fingers laced themselves around her waist and she felt his cheek rub against the springy top of her head. She couldn't move; she didn't even try. Her stomach was turning somersaults.

"God, I've been wanting to do this," he muttered huskily. "Ever since that night on the beach. Shh. Don't say a word. Look." He turned with her in his arms to face the corner. "You see, no bed."

"A hammock!" she exclaimed. "You mean you sleep in it?"

"You find that surprising?"

The hammock swayed in time to the motion of the waves under the boat. It was made of Persian carpeting with tassels at either end. Colored cushions and a woolen throw rug, patterned in a rainbow of blues, emerald and purple, were heaped invitingly on top. By contrast the rest of the room with its simple chest of drawers, cane chair and single flaring piece of driftwood on the wall looked almost Spartan.

She craned her head back with an expression of delight. "I'd have recognized it anywhere. Just what you'd expect to find in the Khan's pleasure dome."

He laughed, rocking her lightly. "All it needs is a few palm fans. Some dancing girls in veils and those trousers they wear. Transparent."

"Diaphanous." She giggled, wondering if he envisioned her in the role. "You don't get seasick lying in there?"

"Want to try it?"

She tensed. "I'll take your word for it."

"Will you?" He sat down on the hammock, still holding her, turning her to face him. His long jean-clad legs were braced on either side as he drew her close between his thighs. "Have you ever lain in one?" he asked softly.

"Not . . . that I remember."

"It's not something you'd forget. It's like . . ." He leaned forward and gravely kissed one dimpled corner of her mouth and then the other. "Being kissed," he finished. His eyes, intent and luminous, held her fast. "Change your mind?"

She shook her head.

He worked her closer, until she was leaning against him, pliant and soft where he was firm and hard. He kissed her again, this time full on the lips with a tender mounting pressure that weakened her knees and worse still, her defences. He slid an arm over her hips, scooped her up from the floor and fell back into the hammock with her. The hammock dipped, tilted, and threatened to dump its cargo out the other side. She shrieked and clutched at him. Laughing, he pressed her tight against his side.

"Lie still. It's all right." He turned his head. With his free hand he smoothed the damp ringlets from her forehead. "Like this, see?"

They lay suspended, lost in a voyage in each other's eyes. She felt on the brink of a discovery. His fingers explored her temples and the soft place under her chin and moved lazily down her throat. She could feel his heart beating fast close to her own. It would be easy, so easy now, to forget he was the man with designs on the cottage, with the power to make or break her ButterCup dream. His hand slipped inside the V neck of her pullover. A tremor like a warning ran through her and she pulled away.

His face on the pillow was flushed, and earnest with tenderness; she had no idea a man could look like that. The rain beat a steady rhythm overhead, heightening the sense of being sheltered and secure. She frowned. It was an illusion, like the look on Rain's face. At any minute, the roof could fall in.

"You're only on probation," she said.

"Can't you trust me?"

"That's just it. I don't know. How can I? What I've had to go on so far—"

"Hasn't exactly inspired confidence. All right. I understand." He lay back, his arm still loosely around her waist, and stared at the skylight. "What exactly is it about me this time?"

She didn't know how to begin.

"Come on. Out with it. Something I said, did, forgot to do—God knows. You have the busiest brain of any woman I've ever met."

"It's nothing like that," she said, stung. "It's just that I couldn't help wondering, all those tables and chairs—the gas grill—"

"The gas grill? You've got my gas grill on your mind at a time like this? I can't believe it." She could sense him drawing away, even though he didn't move, as though he were closing a door, pulling down blinds, leaving her on the outside. "Are you always on the defensive like this?" he demanded. "I've got rights, too."

She was filled with consternation. This wasn't what she wanted, either. If only she'd kept the wretched grill out of it. "Oh, Rain," she whispered.

"Buckets of it," he rumbled. "On the roof. When it's really bad—" he paused, and the hint of a smile worked its way into his tone "—the skylight leaks."

On cue, a rapid succession of drops pattered down on her head. "Oh you!" she gasped and swung her feet to the floor.

OUT OF BREATH, she arrived on her front porch. No wonder she was soaked to the skin. The umbrella Rain had thrust into her hand as an afterthought had two broken spokes and a slashed crown. Typical. She let it fall and fished in her pocket for the key. With it came the invoice she had picked up on his office floor.

She looked over her shoulder with a groan. She could scarcely see the boat; the raindrops were literally bouncing off the road. Returning the invoice would just have to wait. Nothing was that urgent. Besides, she had the flan to put together. And there was the lawnmower, still out on the lawn, turning rusty before her eyes. She stuffed the invoice back into her pocket and promptly forgot about it.

All the next day it drizzled. Puddles appeared on the road and the mountains wrapped themselves in gray cloud. By six-thirty her little foyer was damp with raincoats and umbrellas. The diners, most of them tourists confined indoors all day, were boisterous. Madame Hebert had hastily recruited Lisette, and the three of them were being run off their feet. Joy was bending over the oven taking out scalloped potatoes au gratin, when Lisette put her small dark head around the door and said breathlessly that a lady and a gentleman were in the foyer asking for her. *Très élégants* they were and furious as hornets, she added giggling.

"Furious? When they've only just got in the door?" Joy passed the oven mitts to Madame Hebert and ran a distracted hand through her hair on her way past the doorjamb mirror. At the reception desk she stopped short. It had always been at the back of her mind that someday he'd show up, out of curiosity if nothing else, so it wasn't a complete shock.

"Brian! How nice!" She went up to him with her hand outstretched; he needn't think she'd been moping over his neglect all these months. The woman at his elbow looked down her nose, even though Joy included her in her smile. Brian, brushing furiously at a pale blue trouser leg, ignored her hand.

"Fine welcome! That redneck neighbor of yours backed his truck into the road in front of me, and the Chrysler ended up in the mud."

"Oh dear. Do you need a tow? I could call—"

"No need. MacCallum—is that his name? MacCallum and a couple of his buddies pushed me out. I gave him a piece of my mind. Bunch of yahoos."

She could imagine. Surely Rain hadn't taken his remarks lying down? It would be a first if he had; she thought it more prudent not to ask. Instead she murmured apologetically. The big table was calling for bread, and from the kitchen came the crash of breaking crockery.

"Elinor, my dear, forgive me," Brian said. "This is Joy Lowry. Miss Lowry used to work for us at Lloyd &

Upshaw's. Joy, Elinor Stevens. We'd like somewhere quiet and a little private..."

"If I'd known what a long drive it would be. And in this depressing rain," put in Elinor peevishly. "Just so we could eat at a café run by a former employee of yours? Really, Brian—"

"Darling, the dinner will be worth it. Trust me."

"Ask if the sherry's dry. If it isn't I don't want any."

Witnessing Brian's embarrassment almost made up for Elinor's insulting tone. She was one of those ash blondes whose hair behaved perfectly in a French knot. She wore a severe black-and-white tunic dress that must have cost a fortune and was totally unsuitable for an informal dinner in the country. Joy murmured again, something soothing she hoped, and led the way past the merrymaking crowd in the dining room to the comparative quiet of the sun room. Thank heaven, it was still empty.

Brian glanced about with visible relief as she pulled out their chairs. The room did look pleasant, with the wicker-shaded hanging lamps casting a warm glow in the rainy dusk. Glass and silver gleamed on butter-yellow linen. Across the road, the lights were going on in La Grosse Grenouille, too—about as close as it ever came to being picturesque. She left Lisette to deal with the big table, held the dustpan while Madame Hebert swept up, and brought her driest sherry and paté maison back to the sun room. She was rewarded by Brian launching into a spate of questions about profit margins. "Showing off," she thought, with a peep at Elinor's bored haughty face. She was glad when someone in the dining room called for more wine. "Take a look at the menu till I get back. The trout is local and fresh today."

When she returned, they were ready to order. Brian waxed enthusiastic about trout, pan fried, and Elinor unbent sufficiently to ask Joy what she did to make her hanging begonias bloom like that. A rumble of male voices interrupted her reply. Rain MacCallum, larger than life in muddy blue denim and work boots, was shepherding three companions across the room.

"Got a table left in there?" he boomed.

She gathered her wits just in time to bar their way. "Rain! What—"

"Some of my old construction crew from B.C. flew in to see how the work situation's shaping up here. Guys, meet my favorite neighbor." He introduced each one by name, but they all looked alike to her: big, shy, overwhelmingly male and out of place. She stood her ground. "Thought I'd treat them to a real home-cooked meal tonight," Rain said, and placing a hand on either side of her shoulders, he moved her casually aside. He grinned down at Brian. "Well, well. If it isn't the fellow with the Chrysler, and his missus. Brian, you said your name was?"

"Brian *Upshaw*. And this is Miss Stevens," said Brian, his features taking on the rigid look Joy knew only too well.

"What's wrong with the home cooking at Le Casse-Croûte?" she hissed.

Rain winked. "Waitress is cuter here," he drawled.

He was doing it on purpose: playing the country redneck to annoy Brian. If she'd had the tray in her hand, she would have bounced it off his head. Fuming, she watched helplessly as the men pushed the two remaining tables together.

"More elbow room this way," said Rain. "We're ravenous as bears and plan to stay till the food runs out. Mind if I light up a cigar, Miss Stevens?"

Two crimson spots appeared in Elinor's pale cheeks and Joy said hastily, "*No* cigars!"

The evening fell rapidly apart after that. She ran out of trout, and the big table had a contest to see who could remember the most verses of "Alouette," first in French and then in English. Every time she went into the sun room, one or other of Rain's men was recalling an anecdote from their construction past and the others were whooping with laughter. Brian's face grew more and more frozen. Elinor was looking daggers at him as well as at the rowdies across the room. Joy caught snatches of Brian's customary dinner conversation, consisting of a detailed analysis of a play they'd seen a few nights earlier.

She had enjoyed those conversations in the past, sitting across a table from him; they had stretched her horizons. But here, tonight, they sounded woefully off base. She felt almost sorry for Elinor. Until, taking away the empty plates, she heard her say, "Oh, shut up, Brian." After that she felt sorry for Brian, a novel sensation that left her thoughtful. She half expected them to get up and leave before dessert, but the peach cobbler was included in the price and she ought to have known Brian better than that. Later, waiting in the foyer for Elinor to return from the ladies' room, Brian said grudgingly, "The café's attractive in a rustic way. I can see you've worked hard at it."

"If you want to wait till the crowd leaves, I could show you the rest of the cottage."

"Well . . . Elinor's tired. She wants to go home."

"Of course."

"She's a buyer for a big chain of fashion boutiques. Very successful."

"More your type," said Joy sweetly.

His pale eyes held hers a fraction of a second. "You're sure this is what you want? I still don't think you're going to make it."

"Why shouldn't she make it?" Rain, with his quick light step, had come up behind them. His companions filed on ahead. "You tasted her cooking. Admit it, a girl like Joy is wasted in a lawyers' outfit."

"I don't see that it's any business of yours, Mr. MacCallum."

"Oh, let's just say I take an interest—" Rain's eyes danced wickedly "—in the cottage."

Elinor chose that moment to reappear and Brian didn't comment. Joy called a guarded goodbye from the porch. Rain stepped out beside her and slipped an arm around her waist in the full glare of the Chrysler's headlights. With an effort, she restrained herself until the car had turned into the road.

"Really, was that necessary?"

"What?" He backed her firmly into the shadows behind the morning glory vine and kissed her. She struggled.

"This! And you coming over. Putting on that phony act." She started to giggle in spite of herself. "Did you see his face? Poor Brian. He'll think...he'll think—"

His lips touched hers with light feathery kisses that made her forget about keeping her guard up. "Is it important to you what Brian Upshaw thinks?" he murmured.

"No. Not anymore." She laughed and realized that she meant it. It was a nice liberating feeling. Her hands slid up around the nape of Rain's neck.

He dipped his head and kissed her again, so thoroughly and delightfully it was worth the entire evening.

CHAPTER SIX

"GIPSY! Lovely to hear from you!" Joy glanced at her watch. 8:30 a.m.—it had to be serious for Gipsy Connors to be awake, never mind on the phone long-distance from Montréal. "Is anything wrong?"

"Everything! My entire world is about to crash. But what did I take you away from? Boeuf Charbonnade? Babas au Rhum?"

Joy grimaced. "Nothing so glamorous. I was sorting laundry in the basement. Is it that rock musician who wants you to go to California with him on a motorcycle?"

"No, worse. Much worse. Joy, this time I'm desperate."

Wasn't she always? Joy sighed. And not only Gipsy. After this week she was beginning to think it was part of the female condition. "What's he like?" she asked.

"Oh, Bruno's divine. A walking dream *and* he's in television. A drama producer, yet. Problem is, he's married—in name anyway—and now his wife's found out and is being absolutely impossible."

"Gipsy! How could you! Remember after that Italian fashion designer, you swore you'd stay away from married men."

"Joy, please. Give me some credit. This is different. No children, and they're already living apart. In fact they've been talking about divorce for years, so it's not as though I'm wrecking anybody's home. It's just that Mrs. B is one of those neurotic women who can't stand to see her husband happy. Anyway, the reason I'm calling is, can I come up and see you?"

"Today, you mean?"

"Yes. For a week or two. I've just got to get away, totally incognito. They both keep phoning me at all hours. The strain is beginning to show in my face and that's fatal!"

Joy frowned. One thing about Gipsy, she was a professional. She never allowed the consequences of her roller coaster love life to interfere with her career. Still...

"A week or two? Gipsy, are you sure this is what you want? I mean you're a city person and Lac Désir is definitely country..."

"I'm sure. Believe me, after the dramatics I've been through, I'd *kill* for peace and quiet."

"It's not peace and quiet, exactly. Ever since Rain— well, this man with—"

"What man?"

"Rain MacCallum. Ever since he moored his houseboat off the beach across the road, you wouldn't believe how the café's taken off."

"Sounds crazy—but wonderful! I can help out. Open wine bottles. Run credit cards through the machine. I do great swans in the napkin department. Just what I need to take my mind off Bruno."

Joy felt herself weaken. Gipsy had to be desperate to offer to work. And she could certainly use the help. "It wouldn't be just swans and wine, though. Have you ever waited on tables?"

"I come from a family of six, remember? I can handle it, as long as you give me a couple of hours off, so I can keep up my tan. Or does it rain all the time up there?''

"No. It's clearing now, as a matter of fact," said Joy, with a glance out the window. At the word "rain," a funny sharp stab had gone through her, and Rain's face, earnest and tender the way it had looked that day under the misty skylight, swam before her. Who was she to lecture when a friend fell in love unwisely? It could happen to her. "Gipsy? Of course you can come. Take the Laurentian autoroute north as far as Sainte Agathe des Monts, and follow the sign to Lac Désir.''

"Joy, you're a lifesaver! I've got a catalogue session at ten, but I'll be up directly after. 'Bye!''

Posing for a big mail-order catalogue firm paid the rent, but Gipsy's face really deserved better. They had known each other since fifth grade, when Gipsy was Geraldine Connors, coltish and skinny to her own short and plump, with no hint of the beauty to come in her high slanting cheekbones and generous mouth. Joy hung up, smoothing the creases out of the slip of paper she had carried upstairs with her when the phone rang.

Luckily for Rain, she'd gone through her pockets before dropping her slacks into the washing machine. What she discovered was the forgotten invoice she'd found on the floor of his office—an invoice that turned out to be from La Boucherie de Lac Désir. Two dozen sirloin steaks, the butcher had written in his careful round hand. Ten pounds of ground beef, four dozen hotdogs. Who was Rain planning to feed? An army? She felt a tingling in her head as everything fell into place: the gas grill, the oversized coffee maker, all the tables and chairs. Scotch and soda certainly wasn't the only thing he planned to serve his prospective clients.

She opened the front door just in time to see his truck disappearing down the road, with Grabber gulping lungfuls of air out the passenger window. Typical of the man: there when she didn't want him, gone when she did. She locked the invoice away with her cash so nothing could happen to it before she had a chance to confront him.

It was the height of the lunch-hour rush when she saw him again. She was charging out of the kitchen balancing a tray of brimming soup bowls when he strolled into the foyer carrying three enormous suitcases. With him was a glowing young woman, makeup case in one hand and a bouquet of buttercups and daisies in the other.

"Gipsy!"

"Joy! What a darling café! And don't you look the part in that French waiter's outfit!"

Gipsy's lilting actors' school voice carried clear through the dining room and out to the sun room. Conversation ceased and heads swiveled to take in the voluminous paisley skirt swirling from slender hips and the black tresses piled artlessly on top of the lovely head.

"I saw them rioting in a field," Gipsy said, handing Joy the flowers and leaning forward to give her a kiss, "and absolutely couldn't resist. Rain says they're wild and nobody cares if you pick them."

"Very thoughtful," murmured Joy, juggling flowers and soup bowls to return the kiss. "Nice you're here, Gipsy, but what—I mean how—" She glanced in bewilderment from her friend to Rain. He was watching Gipsy with an expression of . . . well, delight. Her heart dipped painfully. She scarcely heard Gipsy's reply.

"My car broke down. You remember my old Mustang that I've been nursing along for years?" She made an engaging face not lost on her audience. "Well, it finally expired, just outside Lac Désir. I would have been absolutely stranded—me with all my luggage—if this fabulous knight errant hadn't ridden up in his black pickup and taken pity on me. Fortunately!"

"Fortunately," echoed Joy. No man ever did anything for Gipsy out of pity. If he'd at least stop *grinning*. "Since the two of you have met, and I've got my hands full, maybe you'd be so good as to take Gipsy's bags upstairs, Rain? The back bedroom."

"Knows his way around already, does he?" murmured Gipsy archly, behind his retreating back.

Joy felt herself blush to the roots of her hair. "No! I mean . . . it's because he used to own the cottage."

Madame Hebert was signaling urgently from the kitchen; the customers waiting for soup were muttering and looking restless. She would have to set Gipsy straight later. She'd do it in no uncertain terms, she promised herself, hurrying into the dining room and trying not to hear Rain's easy laughter in response to one of Gipsy's comments.

He took his time coming back down. Most of the diners had gone on to coffee and rhubarb Jonathan. Out of the corner of her eye, Joy saw him cross the foyer. She put down the coffeepot.

"Rain? I want to talk to you."

"No need to thank me. Anything for a friend."

"I wasn't intending to thank you. I'm sure Gipsy did that adequately herself. I want to ask you about something."

He cocked a malicious eyebrow, his hand on the door. "More questions about my gas grill?"

"As a matter of fact, yes. Your grill does enter into it. Remember—I have the busiest brain of any woman you've ever met? Well, this time it isn't just in my brain." She didn't attempt to keep the angry scorn out of her tone. "Will you be at the boat when I'm through here?"

"Sure. In the galley." He yanked the door open. "You know the way."

She turned to find Gipsy eyeing her from the foot of the stairs. "Was that my fault? That little contretemps?"

Joy shook her head. When the lump in her throat had subsided sufficiently, she asked, "Have you had lunch?"

"Have you? If not, I'll wait. You look as though you should eat with a friend."

Half an hour later, they sat facing each other across the corner table in the sun room, sharing the last of the salade niçoise and a fresh pot of coffee. Hollyhocks had taken over from the peonies, blooming in delicate shades of rose and ivory outside the screen, and up on the hill the wind tossed in the pines. Joy passed the bread basket.

"I don't know what got into me. Just tired, I guess. You're the one who needs a shoulder."

"Oh..." Gipsy picked at the green beans. "It can wait. What I've got isn't going to go away." Joy looked at her; the flash of bitterness wasn't like Gipsy. Neither was the reticence. This latest romance of hers had to be serious.

"What about the Mustang? Can it be fixed?"

"No. Rain looked under the hood and said it was lucky I wasn't killed. He stopped by the garage in Lac Désir and asked them to tow it away. What a gorgeous man! If it weren't for Bruno..." She left the sentence unfinished. Her appetite seemed to be recovering.

"Imagine finding a treasure like that way up here. Living in a houseboat of all places. Have you been inside?"

"Yes, I have," said Joy, thinking for no good reason of the hammock. "I'm sure he'll ask you over."

"You think so?" The long jade eyes were speculative. "No ring on his finger, I noticed. You're interested in him, aren't you?"

Her heart started to hammer. "Interested is one thing. But where do you go from there? Oh Gipsy—" She stopped, put down her fork and raised tormented eyes. "Rain MacCallum and his houseboat have been nothing but trouble since the moment they got here. I wish I'd never laid eyes on either of them."

"You don't mean that, Joy. Face it. You're in love with him."

The room was so quiet she could hear the waves breaking on the beach. "In love! If you knew what he—"

"Makes no difference what they're like!" Gipsy waved an airy hand. "Men look at us, and we fall in love. Joy, darling, it's me you're talking to. I *know*. I read it in your face the minute we walked in the door."

Joy drew herself up. She crossed her knife and fork on the plate and folded her napkin. "You're wrong. I'm attracted, I'll admit, but no—this time you're wrong." She patted her friend's hand. "You said his name is Bruno and he's a television producer. Tell me the rest."

"Okay. If you say so." Gipsy arched a black brow and pushed her cup in Joy's direction. "Got any more coffee? This may take a while."

"Of course." She stole a glance at her watch as she tipped the coffeepot. Rain would just have to wait. Maybe by now he'd noticed that the invoice was missing and had put two and two together. Fine, she decided, let *him* do a little stewing for a change. Besides, she needed time for Gipsy's disturbing pronouncement to fade.

Of course it did no such thing. It flashed into the forefront of her mind the instant she laid eyes on him. He was stowing packages in the freezer, on the little deck outside the galley. The Dutch door stood ajar and she had simply let herself in and followed the sounds. He turned, straightening up to his full height. He still had on the slim fawn trousers and brown shirt he'd worn into town that morning. He'd had his hair cut and his beard was newly trimmed so that it curled soft and glossy above his open collar. If he'd opened his arms, she would have walked straight into them.

But he didn't. He looked at her, waiting for her to make the first move, his eyes unreadable. The blinds were down, she thought bleakly, and the impulse to reach out for him faded. A good thing, too, she reminded herself tartly, unfolding the invoice. To her dismay, she noticed her hands were trembling. She thrust the paper in front of him.

"I suppose this is what you're putting in the freezer right now?"

He gave the invoice a casual glance. "I wondered where it got to."

"You'll need it for tax purposes, I imagine. It was on the floor of your office the day I was here."

Their eyes met. For an instant she thought his might soften. Then his gaze shifted. A half smile quirked the full lips under the shapely mustache.

"And you couldn't resist a little espionage work. A chance to see what the enemy was up to."

Her color heightened. "It wasn't like that. I saw that the wind had blown a piece of paper off your desk. I picked it up just as you called me, and then I forgot about it. I came across it in my slacks pocket today."

"And? What conclusion did you jump to?"

"That you plan to serve a lot of people a lot of meals."

"Correction. A lot of barbecues."

His offhand tone stung; so did the casual way he went back to sorting packages.

"That must be some promotional tour you give your customers."

"Prospective customers." He shrugged and dropped a package into the freezer. "Every bit helps."

"I'll bet. Do you provide a menu? Is it prix fixe or à la carte?"

"No charge. 'Just come on out for an evening and enjoy yourselves, folks.' That's how it's done in business."

She tightened her lips, seething. "Not in my business. I suppose you don't give a darn that what you're doing is unfair competition to...to established restaurants?"

He leaned against the freezer, his coffee-dark eyes fixed on a sailboat tacking from behind the island. "On the Fraser," he said musingly, "you could travel for miles without seeing so much as a chip wagon. It was pack your own or go hungry."

She clenched her fists. "This isn't the Fraser." Angrily, she moved to the railing. Water slapped against the hull. All day the sun had played hide and seek with the clouds. A brisk wind whipped the crests of the waves into sparkling whitecaps. The sailboat, heeled over to one side, moved with incredible speed. "Do I have to remind you that you're anchored a hundred feet from the front door of the ButterCup Café?'' On the word *ButterCup* her voice cracked, like a child's, and she could have bitten her tongue.

He touched her sleeve. ''You're still wearing your lunch-shift garb. Couldn't wait to hustle over here and sock it to me, could you?''

She spun around, but he was waiting for her. He put his hands on her smooth black-chino hips and with a single look quelled the angry words tumbling in her brain. ''Do you think I'd really offer free lunches on your front step? What do you think I am? A total jerk?'' The blinds were up now, the eyes behind them black with fury. ''If you'd for once take the trouble to find out the facts before going off half-cocked, you might be surprised.''

She took his hands and wrenched them forcibly away. She didn't know how it was possible to be so angry with someone and still find his touch so disturbingly provocative. ''Surprised! I'm constantly surprised, Mr. MacCallum! By everything you do! That's the problem.''

''What problem?'' With an effort he brought his voice down from a shout. ''I take on my passengers, start the engine, disconnect the cables and sail across the lake. To someplace peaceful and quiet where we can eat our hamburgers without fear of attack by jealous café proprietors. You don't even have hamburgers on the menu, damn it!''

''Jealous? Of this...barge and a few charred hamburgers? Is that what you think?''

''Well? Aren't you? Admit it. What you're really asking is for me to show up at your door, cap in hand.

'Please, Miss Lowry. Could you fit my prospective clients into your crowded seating schedule?'"

Color flooded her face. She wouldn't have put it that bluntly, even to herself, but yes, maybe there was something like that at the back of her mind. "I do run a restaurant," she muttered, "and you *are* just across the road."

"So you keep reminding me. As if I needed reminding." He sounded tired. It occurred to her that he probably wished the ButterCup halfway across the Laurentians as fervently as she wished the same of La Grenouille. The thought made her feel worse instead of better.

"Let me remind *you*," he said. "My business is to get people to buy houseboats. To do that, they have to enjoy being on them. Not sitting across the road, talking about it."

Joy felt sure he wished *she* were halfway across the Laurentians, too. "I suppose, if the barbecues are part of a cruise, it'll be all right." Face a careful blank, she eyed him. He eyed her back, his expression a replica of hers.

"So," he said crisply, "now we've got that settled, can I get back to my work?"

"Of course." She stood there, her back against the rail, gripped by the most senseless longing for a cup of Russian tea in a wicker-nested glass.

He tossed a package into the freezer, where it landed with a thud. "I wouldn't want to keep you," he said. "I'm sure you have potatoes to whip. Strawberries to mash. Whatever."

"Oh. It won't be so hectic at the café anymore. Now that my friend—"

He looked up. Sunlight danced and quivered on his face. "Right. Gipsy Connors. The model, someday-to-be-actress." He showed his teeth at their most dazzling. "Now there's a girl a man could rob banks with."

And *she* wasn't, supposed Joy. "Gipsy and I go back a long way," she informed him stiffly. "It was...decent of you to help her out."

"Oh, decency had nothing to do with it. Believe me."

How could he be so blatant? After the way he'd looked at her in the hammock. This new wolfish side of Rain was one she hadn't experienced before. "Gipsy already has a man in her life," she said coldly.

"Is that why she's up here alone? Maybe she needs a little diversion. A new interest to take her mind off the old, so to speak."

"Certainly not!" Was he serious? She couldn't tell. She drew herself up. "She'll tell you herself. You can do as you please."

"I always do, don't I?" he said, in the velvet tone that made her skin prickle. He bent over his packages as though she wasn't there.

She turned on her heel and walked back the way she had come, through the galley and the big empty lounge where the timbers creaked with each movement of the boat. His voice stopped her at the door.

"Joy!"

Even when he said her name like that, impersonally, it made her go weak at the knees. She waited.

His head appeared in the pass-through, hair rumpled by the wind. "Just wanted to let you know I'm giving a party a week from Saturday. A sort of kickoff for MacCallum Houseboats—inviting some of my suppliers and the big marina and resort-hotel owners from around the Laurentians. There'll be live music and dancing and it'll go on till quite late. You and your friend might as well come."

She frowned. A slow anger began to take over from the numbing sense of powerlessness she'd felt until now. "Is that supposed to be an invitation?"

"I told you next time I gave a party, I'd invite the neighbors. Come around nine. Wear something glamorous—"

"Diaphanous?" she suggested bitterly.

An expression passed over his face, too quickly for her to read. "Sure. If you think that's your style."

He could have been talking to a stranger; worse, somebody he had no liking or respect for. Maybe he was goading her in the hope she'd say no. Then she would have no right to complain when the dance music kept her awake and the Cadillacs backed over her marigolds. Well, he could have spared himself the effort. She wouldn't come to his party if he dragged her.

"Maybe it slipped your mind. I work Saturday nights."

"Come late. You won't be missed in the crowd." His tone was cavalier.

"I don't accept invitations to places where I won't be missed. Besides, I'm opening for brunch Sundays, so I'll need my sleep."

He grinned and gave her an insolent, little wave. "Good luck!"

She would have flown across the room and punched him if she hadn't been afraid of what getting that close to him might do to her.

"I'll bet your friend Gipsy doesn't refuse."

"Ask her yourself. I'm not her social secretary."

"I plan to."

"Fine."

She let herself out and slammed the Dutch door behind her. They were like children, each topping the other in remarks intended to pierce and draw blood. Only they were not children, and it wasn't a game. What had *happened* to them, she thought, scrambling awkwardly onto the gangplank. She could see him still watching, his eyes gleaming. "Call yourself a builder? You still haven't put up a step here. I hope one of your bigtime marina operators breaks a leg," she called over her shoulder.

A shout of laughter sped her on her way. She marched up the wharf with what she hoped was a fine careless dignity, although everything in her cried out to run.

"The enemy" he'd called her; or no, he'd called himself the enemy. Her mind was in no shape to analyze the distinction. Was that how he saw them now, as enemies? How had it come to this? She would have given anything to hear his big light step on the planks behind her. Instead there was only the sound of waves crashing onto the shore.

If only she didn't love him, she thought, and stood stock-still on the sand.

Gipsy hadn't been wrong. She *was* in love, deeply and fully in love with tough, tender, exasperating Rain MacCallum. All this time, while they'd been sparring about houseboats and the cottage and he'd been driving her around the bend, love had been sneaking up on her. No wonder the mere thought of him filled her with such yearning, such a seesaw of emotions. It wasn't fair, she thought, gazing stormily at the houseboat. The striped awnings were lit up by a shaft of sunlight so that it looked like a circus tent. She let out a long explosive breath. Now what was she supposed to do?

THE NEXT MORNING, La Grosse Grenouille was gone.

Joy slid back the door and stepped barefoot onto the balcony, unable to believe her eyes. Nothing but water lay on either side of the wharf: tiny silver wavelets, rosily streaked with dawn, lapping peacefully at the shore. She thought of all the awful, wounding things they'd said to each other yesterday and wondered for one wild instant if she'd succeeded in wishing the houseboat away overnight. But of course she didn't really wish that, it would mean Rain—her hand flew to her mouth. Where was Rain?

"Joy! Joy! Are you awake?"

Gipsy came running up the stairs full tilt. "Joy! You won't believe this. Take a look outside—" She burst into the bedroom. "Oh, you have!" She joined Joy on the balcony, attractively disheveled in a lace nightdress and tumble-down hair. "What happened to it? Do you know? Any idea?"

Joy shook her head. The truck was still there. Maybe he'd slipped away for a test sail across the lake. But in the dark?

"I couldn't sleep anymore—too much noise. Birds yelling—" Gipsy knit her brow. "What *are* those birds with the rusty vests and mean little shoebutton eyes?"

"Robins?"

"Robins. Anyway, I went downstairs to watch the sun come up—can you believe I haven't seen a sunrise since I was nine, in Brownie camp—and when I looked out the window, the houseboat was gone." She stared at Joy and lowered her voice. "You don't think it sank, do you?"

A chill ran the length of Joy's spine. She clutched the neck of her thin cotton nightgown. "It couldn't have. The water's not deep enough near the shore." All the same, she found herself peering down at the water, as though it might reveal a murky shimmer of green, or the stovepipe sticking up.

"Maybe it drifted out a ways and then—" Gipsy hesitated. "I mean, that was some wind last night."

Joy had heard it too, for what seemed like hours, while she lapsed in and out of restless dreams of Rain. She'd heard it lashing the waves and rattling the roof in sudden gusts, so that she'd worried about the shingles, and roaring like an express train through the pines on the hill. But a man who'd sailed a houseboat on the Fraser wasn't likely to let it sink under him in Lac Désir. Maybe La Grosse Grenouille had simply left the way it had come, by road; maybe he'd had it all arranged. No, that idea was even sillier. Gipsy was right; the houseboat's disappearance had to be the fault of the wind.

"Look at those cables dangling in the water. Ripped out, aren't they?" she said, echoing Joy's thoughts. They scanned the lake and every foot of shoreline they could see, but there was no sign of the houseboat. It was a beautiful morning, everything dewy and fresh, with the sun rising innocently over the mountains. Church bells pealed across the bay from Lac Désir for early-morning Mass.

"Maybe we should call the Sûreté de Québec. Just in case," said Joy, turning reluctantly indoors.

Gipsy patted her arm. "Don't worry. He's all right. A man like Rain can handle anything."

She'd known him precisely one day, and already her confidence in him was unshakeable. Joy shook her head; amazing, the effect Rain had on women. She slipped into her dressing gown and started down the stairs. Somebody was pounding on the front door. It wasn't even seven o'clock yet. Couldn't anybody read signs anymore? Face set in a chilly frown, she thrust back the bolt.

Rain stood on the porch, wet clothes plastered to his tall frame and a sheepish grin on his face. "Hi, neighbor. Did I wake you?"

"Rain!" she gasped. She felt herself go hot and cold. A smile of joyful relief lit up her features before she could stop it. She couldn't stop her hand, either, from reaching out and touching him to make sure he was real and not just a leftover from her dreams.

"Mmm, nice welcome. For a change. You wouldn't possibly have a coffee to go with that?"

She drew back, reining in her runaway emotions. "I was just about to make some," she said primly. "Come in. It's just that I thought—I mean Gipsy thought—maybe you were—"

"Drowned?" He cocked an eyebrow. "Kind of you—Gipsy, that is—to be concerned."

"What happened? Where's the houseboat? You're dripping wet. Even your boots—" She glanced disapprovingly at the puddles following him across the hardwood floor of the foyer. She tried not to sound hopeful. "The boat didn't sink, did it?"

He shook the hair out of his eyes, scattering water like a wet dog. "Sink? MacCallum houseboats don't sink. Mooring lines broke in the storm. She drifted over to the other side of the island. Grounded on a rock. I swam to shore and hitched a ride back here."

She bit back the words of shocked commiseration and awe that sprang to mind. "Isn't that a bit careless? Losing a houseboat in a windstorm? Couldn't you have started the engine? I mean instead of drifting around like that?"

"Sure. If I'd realized. But I was fast asleep." He winked. "Thing is, with a hammock you get used to the rocking. I didn't wake up till she was grounded." He reached across the reception desk, his sleeve dripping on the menus. "All right if I use your phone?"

She snatched the menus to safety and got him some towels from the washroom. He was dialing when she came back. "I don't want her springing a leak. I'll need a good strong tow and some of my men. I wonder who I can rouse this early. *Allô, chez Yves?* Yes, wake him for me, *s'il vous plaît.*"

She slipped into the kitchen to see about coffee. Gipsy, nominally decent in an orange silk wrapper, had already plugged in the coffee maker and was getting out eggs and a frying pan. "Too bad we can't lend him any clothes. He'll need a good hot breakfast. The least we can do to help." She gave Joy a winning smile and handed her the spatula. "If you fry the eggs, I'll make the toast."

"Eggs? Toast? Let's not get carried away—"

"Joy, darling! Declare a truce! You wouldn't begrudge a man in his condition some nourishment? He could die of hypothermia."

Shamed, Joy took the spatula. She was being petty and mean and it wasn't like her. Rain was replacing the receiver when she went in to tell him coffee and eggs were ready in the kitchen.

"The show's on the road," he said, rubbing his hands like a man who'd just organized a Sunday-school picnic. He got up to follow her, leaving a wet patch on the stool. "Yves and a bunch of the others are on their way. We think we can get hold of a man with a forty horsepower boat. Nobody's had breakfast yet, so I told them come on over to the ButterCup first. Okay?"

She stifled a shriek and glanced down at her dressing gown and fuzzy slippers. "When?"

"Five minutes. Ten." He grinned. "Isn't this your morning-shift uniform?"

She glared at him. Yesterday's hurt and anger still simmered below the surface. She had tried to make allowances, but this was the limit. "The ButterCup's good enough for you today, is it? How handy for you!"

He shrugged. "We could always go to Le Casse-Croûte. Only I happen to know the cute waitress is on holiday." His eyes roved boldly over her frilly pink curves. "Quit worrying. You look fine to me. Just what a man likes to see first thing in the morning."

She blushed and fled up the stairs.

It was chaos half the morning. Rain held court in the sun room, planning his operation and waiting for the forty horsepower man. Men in rubber boots clumped in and out, squealing trucks and cars raised dust in the parking lot, the telephone rang off the desk. The coffee maker worked nonstop and she ran out of eggs. Gipsy was in her element, charming every male in sight.

"Is it always like this?" she asked, when the last of them had left in the power boat. "I'll be able to forget Bruno in a week."

"Don't count on it," muttered Joy. The morning had only heightened her own painful knowledge that she was hopelessly in love and quite helpless to deny Rain anything, however inconvenient. She was in the kitchen, way behind schedule with all the mess still to clean up and the chicken Dijon to prepare for that night, when Gipsy yelled, "Here she comes. Wow!"

La Grosse Grenouille's snub green nose rounded the island. Startlingly large, and shaped like a squat frog, she nevertheless managed to glide regally over the sparkling water. Some of her awnings were torn, but her fleur-de-lis still flew. Joy allowed herself to be pulled down to the wharf to see the houseboat dock. She could hear the steady chug-chug of the diesel engine and see Rain looking triumphant in the little wheelhouse tucked into the prow. The men lounged about on the decks. Grabber, none the worse for wear, pushed his big wedge-shaped head through the rail and grinned. A cheer went up as Rain maneuvered the boat deftly alongside the wharf, enabling the men to spring across and secure the cables.

"I COULDN'T HAVE done it without you," he said, half an hour later, after everyone else had gone home.

"Without me? Or without my telephone and the café?"

Rain laughed and brushed a smudge of mustard from her chin in a gesture that was endearingly familiar. "That's my Joy. Always on the alert in case I pull a fast one."

"I'm not your Joy."

"No," he said evenly. "You're not, are you?"

If only she were! She felt suddenly depressed. "And your record for pulling fast ones is excellent."

Their eyes met and held. Then his slid away and his grin mocked her. "Keep them guessing," he said. "That's my motto. Well…" He pushed open the screen door. "I'm off to swab the decks. This little misadventure proved one thing, though."

"Oh?"

"Yes." Satisfaction warmed his voice. "The Bull-frog's engine works like a charm. I think I'll run the first demonstration cruise tomorrow."

She bent over the chicken without answering. The truce was over.

CHAPTER SEVEN

MADAME HEBERT slapped the neatly trimmed chops onto the grill, one-two-three, and cleared her throat.

"There ought to be a law."

"Well, there isn't. I called City Hall and the clerk told me they have no regulations covering houseboats."

"All the same, the mayor should not permit it. Those barbecue cruises are going to put you out of business."

Joy looked up from the ruby-red new beets she was scrubbing in the sink. Even her smile felt tired. "It's called free enterprise."

She didn't blame Madame Hebert for feeling put out. This was the first time in a week Joy had required her services. From the day Rain MacCallum had posted the big green sign stating Demonstration Houseboat Cruises—Barbecue Gratis, business at the ButterCup had plummeted like the temperature in January. At first she'd managed to hold on to the lunch-hour crowd, then Rain had come up with a noon cruise to take care of the overflow from his evening trips. She got used to seeing cars pull into her parking lot and spill out people, only to have them stroll across the road to the houseboat. Some of them put their heads in the door long enough to cancel reservations. The party of six for tonight was pretty safe, she meditated gloomily.

"My wife's afraid of water," the voice on the telephone had laughingly informed her.

She set aside the beets and leafed through her recipe file. There had to be some way of making beets sound exciting on a menu. Maybe Rain wasn't actively trying to put her out of business, but she doubted he was losing any sleep over the prospect, either. Why should he? If she couldn't meet her mortgage payments, he'd be first in line to buy the cottage from her. The way things were going, that should be happening just in time for the October freeze up.

Still brooding, she left Madame Hebert to deal with the mixed grill and trailed upstairs to change. A dazzling flash of blue and white caught her eye. The kingfisher was diving in a patch of yellow pond lilies that had somehow survived Rain's depredations. She watched the bird fly up to the birch tree with a silver minnow in its beak and shivered. A month ago she would have been glad for the bird; now she felt sorry for the fish. Rain would be getting ready for his evening cruise now, she thought, fastening the buttons on her cotton eyelet blouse. She hadn't decided yet whether it hurt more to watch him on the houseboat, moving chairs and lugging cases of soft drinks, or to deliberately stay away from the balcony, knowing he would be down there.

He wasn't on the deck this time. Eye-catching in nautical white, he was sauntering across the road, Grabber loping at his heels. Probably fetching something or other from the garage—he was constantly turning up in the yard, acting as though he already owned the place. And the mess! Some days she could hardly back the Honda out of the garage. She was going to have to talk to him about it. Some time when she felt sure that one look from his eyes wasn't going to reduce her to teenaged helplessness. Just as she came to this decision, she saw Grabber launching himself down the flagstone path.

JS! He'd been sunning himself on the porch, she remembered, and she plunged onto the balcony in time to see the cat shinnying up a post, ears flattened for speed. Grabber bounced up and down below like a furious white rubber ball, barking his frustration. Joy looked for a loose object, rejected a potted geranium, and hurled her slipper. End over end it hurtled, straight at Rain's head advancing up the path. He sidestepped and caught it neatly, laughing.

"Wicked curve! Does the Lac Désir ball team know about you?"

She waited for the floor to open up and swallow her, but it didn't. "I was never any good at games," she muttered.

"So I see." He held up the ridiculous bit of pink fluff. "Size six? Five?" he marveled. "If that. Here!" He tossed it lightly back to her. His sparkling eyes pinned her to the spot. Her heart started to pound.

"If you wouldn't mind," she managed to say, "calling off your beast?"

"Grabber! Heel!" he ordered, and a shiver ran down her spine. It was a tone no dog could afford to disobey and Grabber didn't try. "Good lord," Rain said, surveying the damage to her juniper shrubs. He had the grace to sound apologetic.

"They'll match the marigolds, anyway," she said coldly. "The group you had on last night's cruise took a short cut to the parking lot."

He swung round to look. His hair had grown since his haircut last week and was starting to curl again at the nape of his neck. She remembered how soft it felt, how it smelled faintly of wood shavings.

"Why didn't you tell me?" he threw at her. "You want me to look like a vandal on top of everything else? Order new ones. Have the nursery bill me."

Nothing was a problem, to hear him tell it. "This may come as a surprise to you," she said, "but there are some things money can't fix. Or buy."

"So I've heard." He gazed up at her inscrutably, the sun on his beard glinting like gold dust. His face had acquired another layer of tan, she noticed. "Have you got five minutes and a coffee?" he asked. "It's time we had a talk."

She frowned. That had been her first mistake, giving him coffee and a chance to talk.

"Hi, handsome! You up there, Joy?" Gipsy craned her neck from the porch steps in a bathrobe and terry cloth turban the scarlet of poppies. The queen of Sheba had nothing on her. "I was washing my hair and I thought I heard voices. Public or private?" she enquired archly.

"The terms haven't been hammered out yet." Rain grinned the way he usually did around Gipsy. "Changed your mind yet, about trying out as social director on the boat?"

Something snapped in Joy's brain. "Why don't the two of you talk? I'm sure you have more to say to each other than Mr. MacCallum and I do." She slid the door shut with a thud, the closest she could come to slamming it.

The evening didn't improve noticeably. Madame Hebert burned the sausages. JS refused to come down off the roof. Rain's cruise was late getting under way and his Rolling Stones drowned out her Mozart. Gipsy, who'd spilled the wine, ended up sitting cozily beside the husband of the woman who was afraid of water.

Finally, Madame Hebert's feet gave out and Joy was obliged to send her home with the leftovers and finish the washing-up herself.

Wearily in bed at last, she hugged the pillow and cried herself to sleep. In the morning she felt drained but calmer. She lettered a sign that read Parking for Café Guests Only, and nailed it to the ButterCup signpost, something she'd been meaning to do for at least a week.

It was Wednesday, her day for shopping. She wandered up and down the aisles of the Supermarché Lac Désir, trying to think up catchy meals that called for a lot of vegetables and a minimum of costly meat. With the start of July and hot weather, the garden had shifted into high gear and she was having trouble keeping up. A buffet might be the answer; she could make a lot of salads—

"Pardon me, pretty lady." She spun round at the tap of a hand on her shoulder and found herself face to face with Rain. "Do you know about cantaloupes?" he asked.

"Oh, hello Rain," she said weakly. "Cantaloupes?"

"Hello yourself," he said softly and a moment of eternity ticked by while she rediscovered his eyes. "About these cantaloupes," he said, in a tone that had nothing to do with melons. "Isn't there some trick to telling when they're ripe?"

"Trick? Oh, yes." Her mind seemed momentarily to have deserted her. "It's simple, really. Place your thumb here—"

"Where?"

"Here." She took his hovering thumb and guided it to the green depression at the end. "Press lightly. If it's soft, and the cantaloupe gives off a fragrance..." Her voice petered out. Through some sleight of hand, her thumb was on the depression and his firm warm hand was covering hers. She felt her knees turn to rubber. Ten days, she thought despairingly, ten days of thinking about his touch had done this to her. She pulled her hand free, asking with passable coolness, "How many do you need?"

"A dozen."

Resentment shot through her and she welcomed it. "Of course. For your prospective clients. Well, the lesson's over." She pretended a consuming interest in new potatoes farther down the aisle. He followed, pushing his cart. Somebody should tell him he looked indecently bare to be out in public, in his cut-off jeans and faded T-shirt.

"The music bother you last night?" he asked.

"Not at all," she lied sweetly. "Mozart needed a little shaking up."

"I suppose we were a bit noisy coming back, too."

"No more than usual. One merrymaker falling off the gangplank. Ten people shouting good-night. Half a dozen cars slamming their doors and revving their engines."

He clutched his head and groaned. "I tell them to keep it down, I really do." He brightened, interposing his grin between her and the potatoes. "At least the junk is off the beach. You've got to admit that."

"Of course it's off the beach. It's all in my garage. Speaking of the garage—" Now was the time to tackle him about it. But he was a jump ahead of her.

"Disaster area, isn't it? I've been meaning to get over there one day..."

"Which day? When? I had to move a pile of shingles this morning to get the Honda out."

He considered, tousled head cocked to one side, eyes dancing. "Didn't I see a new notice out there? Parking punishable by death, or something? Maybe we could work out a deal."

Typical. She defended her rights and he took it as a personal affront. Or even worse, a joke. She scowled. "What kind of deal?"

"I'll clean up the garage if you restore my parking privileges."

"What! One has nothing to do with the other. A landlord has the right to expect a tenant to keep the premises neat."

"It's not in the lease."

Outrage hardly described what she felt. "Neither is parking!" She wheeled her cart briskly down to pet foods. He was right behind her. "Impasse?" she heard him say softly. Her heart did a loop. The last time that word had come up, he'd put his arms around her and kissed her. And now? They were fighting it out in a supermarket. She clattered half a dozen cans of Cat's Whiskers into the cart.

"I'll be perfectly frank with you," he said. "You've got me at your mercy. Without the use of your lot, I'm up the creek. A fully booked cruise requires at least—"

"You expect me to care? Maybe you should build a five-story parking garage on the beach and be done with it!" She swung around the corner of the aisle into health-care products before he could answer.

SHE THOUGHT she had shaken him off, but there he was, waiting for her beside the Honda, surrounded by Supermarché bags and a basket of cantaloupes. He was leaning against the hood, one bronzed leg crossed over the other, whistling a Bruce Springsteen tune. She trudged across the parking lot with her load, conscious of his eyes taking in the motion of her hips under the cotton folds of her flaring apricot skirt.

"Now what?" she snapped, ignoring the funny things her breathing was doing.

He jerked his curly chin toward the truck parked farther down the row. "Flooded the engine. Battery's dead."

"So?"

He gave her the benefit of his smile, wide and guileless. "I thought you might graciously offer to give me a lift to the garage."

Did she have a choice? "All these bags and the basket, too?" she asked curtly.

"Can't leave them broiling in the truck."

Grudgingly she unlocked the door and they stowed their purchases in the back. "That's all you bought?" he asked, folding his big frame adroitly into the space beside her, so close she caught his fresh sun-warmed scent.

"That's all I need." A torrent of accusation beat against her brain. But she'd sworn to herself that she wouldn't give him the satisfaction. She turned the key in the ignition and glanced over her shoulder. Out of the corner of her eye she could see his face, quiet and intent.

"Light suppers at the ButterCup this week?"

"Buffet." She steered the Honda into rue Principale and threw him a challenging look. "As in 'Stop for a buffet on your way to the cruise.'"

"I see." She saw his upper lip begin to lift under the silky bristles of his mustache. "If you can't beat 'em, join 'em. Is that it?"

She didn't answer. If she said one word, she'd un-
leash them all. Damn him.

She slowed for tourists in front of the graceful white
church. Sunlight dazzled on the steep silver roof, and
pink and white petunias bloomed in the big circular bed
out front; Fleurs de Saint Joseph, the local people called
them. She saw that L'Artisanat, the craft shop, had put
out tables with a display of hand-woven mats and the
little carved wooden habitant figures tourists loved to
buy. Next door, Le Casse-Croûte, freshly painted and
with a new neon sign, was doing brisk business. A
breath of air stirred the flags at city hall—where they
didn't have any rules covering houseboats. Color glinted
and glowed everywhere, contrasting with the stark gray
of Joy's mood.

"That wasn't very nice back there, that crack about
building a parking garage on the beach." Rain slewed
himself round to look at her, eyes veiled under dark
lashes. "How come I get the feeling I can't do anything
right anymore, where you're concerned?"

"Do you care?"

"Should I? You tell me."

Don't you know? Can't you see? she thought with
sudden anguish. If he didn't, she certainly couldn't tell
him. She turned off onto rue d'Érables and he put out
his hand.

"Stop here a minute?"

"But the garage—it's another two blocks..."

"I'll phone them from here." She had scarcely slowed
down and already he had the door open.

"And your groceries?"

"Wait for me. I'll be right back."

He ran back to the delicatessen at the corner and took
the steps two at a time. All along the street, maples

shaded the neat white, typically Québecois houses, with wrought iron staircases curving to meet second-story verandahs in the way she usually found so delightful, but now hardly saw. Everything, yet nothing, had changed between them. He was ruining her livelihood, making her emotional life a torment, and still she couldn't say no to the man. Through a gap in a cedar hedge she gazed across a lawn edged with white, mauve and crimson cosmos, airy as butterflies, down to the lake shimmering in the sun. Sailboats danced on the water in a gay holiday scene, their sails making snowy triangles against the humped woolly backdrop of the mountains. She shut off the engine and rolled down the window as far as it would go. It was getting hotter by the minute. She caught a glimpse of herself in the outside mirror, hair rioting in damp gold ringlets and freckles standing out on her nose. She'd been having trouble sleeping and it showed in the dark patches under her eyes. Butterscotch eyes, she thought with a little stab. Where was he, anyway?

He could have made three phone calls by now. Serve him right if she drove off and left him—left his groceries too, sitting on the curb. But the thrifty cook in her recoiled at the thought. When he emerged, he was carrying two more bags and a box of pastry. Frowning, she leaned over to open the door.

"A call to the garage, you said. I'm not playing chauffeur so you can run errands."

"No sweat." He hoisted himself onto the seat. "The line was busy. We've got to talk, you and I," he added, out of the blue. She paid no attention and took off down the street.

"Take the next right," he said. "Up the hill."

"That's the old road to the Auberge des Vents. Why—"

He leaned across and wrenched the wheel to the right.

"What do you think you're doing?" she gasped.

"I told you. We've got to talk. And not back at the café or the boat. On neutral ground. If you won't drive, I'll remove you bodily from the driver's seat and do it myself."

She glanced at his tight-lipped profile; he was quite capable of carrying out his threat. Anger made a knot in her stomach that was part excitement, because of Rain. The washboard gravel road wound higher and higher. Wild raspberry bushes billowed over the fields and thrust out thorny arms to scratch the fenders; it was obvious nobody drove up here anymore. She stopped the car as soon as the Auberge came in sight and got out. Rain could make his way on his own. She waded through knee-high grass spangled with aromatic white yarrow and purple vetch, and loud with crickets.

It was seven years since that last summer she'd been here with Aunt May. The tall arched casement windows of the Auberge had stood open to the hilltop breezes that gave the inn its name; now they were closed and shuttered. Paint peeled from white verandah columns and one of the wide shallow steps had rotted through. Stepping over it, she found a shutter that had worked loose. Shading her eyes, she peered in at the lounge, an enormous high-ceilinged room with a stone fireplace at one end and shrouded furniture standing in ghostly groups.

They'd held Saturday night dances in this room, the summer she was seventeen. They'd pushed the chairs and tables back and the musicians had tied *ceintures fléchés*, the traditional woven red sashes of old Québec, over their white slacks. She had worn her hair long then, and there'd been young men. No one that she particularly remembered, but often she'd stayed till the last dance, long after a smiling Aunt May, watching over coffee, had slipped away to bed. Inexplicably, Joy's eyes filled with tears. She turned blindly away from the window and found herself encircled by two strong arms.

"Oh Rain," she whispered brokenly against the comforting wall of his chest. "It was Aunt May's last summer and I didn't know."

His arms tightened and she felt the touch of his lips on her hair. "I'm sorry, Joy," he murmured. "I should have realized, bringing you up here..."

He was feeling sorry for her—the last thing she wanted. She didn't normally act in such a weepy manner. Maybe the fact that she hadn't been exactly happy lately had something to do with it. She pulled free of his arms and fumbled in her skirt pocket for a handkerchief. "I'm all right now, really."

He picked up the deli bags he'd dropped on the steps. "Lunch," he said firmly. "And then we'll talk." She didn't protest; for once she was glad to let him take charge. He steered her across the remnants of the lawn to a mossy outcropping of rock. Through the birches and young spruce trees below, blue as an eye, winked the lake. Beyond it the mountains, shading from green to blue then to violet and smoke in the hazy distance, climbed fold upon fold into the sky.

She smiled faintly. "You remembered the view."

"It's not one you forget," he said, giving her a side-long glance. "Désir du Coeur. You know what it means, don't you?"

She turned toward him and nodded, her chest suddenly tightening. "Desire of the heart." It took a minute for their eyes to disengage.

She perched on the rock, while he spread out the contents of the bags. Montréal smoked meat on caraway rye; dill pickles and potato salad in takeout containers. Pumpernickel rolls and a wedge of Québec's own pungent Oka cheese. A bottle of Beaujolais thrust into a plastic bucket of ice, and long-stemmed plastic wineglasses. The pastry. She stared; she'd had no idea.

He whipped a dinner-sized napkin onto her lap and handed her a paper plate with the word Limoges centered in a green and gold rim. She smiled in spite of herself.

"Exactly how long have you been planning this spur-of-the-moment kidnapping?"

He uncorked the wine with a Swiss Army knife and poured it. "Since I saw your face."

"My...face?"

He handed her the glass, then leaned over and wiped the trace of a tear from her cheek with his knuckle. "You've been sleeping too little. Worrying too much."

She frowned into her wine. Just because she'd succumbed to a moment's weakness over Aunt May, he needn't think she was going to go all soft and vulnerable. "I haven't done anything of the sort," she lied, prim-lipped.

Half his smoked meat disappeared at a bite. "You always spend your nights with the light on?"

"Are you saying you spy on me?"

He shrugged, saw she wasn't eating, and thrust a sandwich into her hand. "It's not spying when you wake up at 4:00 a.m. with a light shining on your face."

"It doesn't!"

"Want to come over and test it some night?"

Color stained her cheeks. If only her eyes weren't constantly drawn to those long bare legs. She had seen legs like that on a Greek statue in the Montréal Art Museum, only these were warm brown flesh. "I fall asleep sometimes, reading," she said defensively.

"Reading your bank statement?" He cocked a provocative eyebrow.

"My bank statement is none of your business."

He crunched a pickle with gusto. "I was under the impression it was. From things you've said. Ad infinitum."

She ate in stubborn silence.

"That bad, is it?" He downed his wine and poured them both a refill. "Go on. Tell me. What am I doing now to sabotage the ButterCup? Besides being a loud, boorish vandal who takes up too much parking space?"

She put down her glass. She hated it when his voice took on that sarcastic tone. "As if you didn't know! Do you honestly believe all those people lined up for cruises are there for the houseboat?"

"And not for the steak? Instead of quiche at the ButterCup—is that what you're saying?"

"Yes. That's what I'm saying."

"Can you prove they're not?"

She was taken aback. "Well, no. I mean, how—"

"Precisely. Maybe I should stand on the gangplank and ask. Sir? Madam? What are your intentions? Honorable or otherwise?" He reached for the pastry box, a coiled spring of impatient energy. "Joy, the point of a dinner cruise is to change people's minds. Sure, people may be attracted to the idea of a free steak, but if the cruise is a pleasant experience, they'll go on to the next step of thinking about buying a boat for themselves. It's simple arithmetic: the more people I get, the more houseboats I'll launch."

She sat in miserable silence, her arms wrapped round her knees. It was hopeless; they were back at square one. He opened the box with a flourish, leaned over and nudged her with it. Butter tarts, her favorite, and miniature rum balls smothered in chocolate sprinkles; her face softened.

"And is it working?" she asked. "Are people buying houseboats?"

"Listen." His shoulder brushed hers as he moved closer. "Six orders already. Signed on the dotted line. I'm lining up construction crews on three lakes."

"I'm glad for you," she said. She was, too, she thought with a kind of wonder. Delighting in his dream, he was like a boy, his face eager and full of warm certainty. They looked at each other. Crickets throbbed on the hillside. A breeze, carrying the scent of roses still blooming somewhere in the tall grass, lifted the hair on his forehead and stirred the ruffled V of her blouse. His eyes moved over her face, to her lips and down, the lashes sinking, to the shadowy swell of her breasts. Heart pounding, she smoothed the ruffles back in place. Gently, he caught her hand and pressed a kiss into her palm. At the touch of his vibrant lips, a white-hot sensation flowed through her. His eyes were forest pools, shot through with sunlight. "I could drown," she thought, frightened by the intensity of her desire, "here and now."

Slowly, tenderly, he took each of her fingertips in turn and pressed them down on her palm, sealing his kiss inside. "There *is* a solution," he murmured. "Every good impasse has one."

"Yes?" Her smile was rueful; she couldn't stop her lips trembling. The houseboat and the café again. If just for once they could explore their relationship without having to worry about competition between his business and hers, she might finally get to know where she stood with him. "If you relocated La Grosse Grenouille. On one of those others lakes..."

He sat very still. "Is that what you want? For me to move?"

"No, not you, Rain." She wasn't saying this right. "Only the houseboat. The cruises—"

"La Grenouille's my home. My living." He dropped her hand and got to his feet with a casualness that hurt more than if he'd slapped her. "I suppose you'd like that. If I packed up and cleared out. Left Lac Désir to you and that damned café of yours. In the cottage my family built—"

She scrambled up and grabbed his arm to make him face her. "And *you* abandoned! To people who used it for a month each summer and didn't put a nickel into it. The roof leaked, the plumbing was hopeless and the lilacs had grown over the windows. You're lucky I came along and salvaged the place!"

It wasn't Rain staring down at her, but some stranger. "Thanks. For reminding me where I stand on the list."

"What list? I haven't told you anything!" she cried out, fighting tears.

"Sure you have. The list in your head that has all your priorities arranged on it: the ButterCup, the mortgage, the parking, the cat... have I missed any?" He scooped up a bag and started tossing things into it. "Tell me something. Simple curiosity—nothing personal. Has any man ever got through to you? Or have you always worn porcupine quills?"

Her chin tilted defiantly. "If by that last remark you mean do I try to protect myself against men who take advantage of me, then yes!"

He eyed her dispassionately. "Learned it from your ex-boyfriend, I suppose. Your boss—that Upshaw guy. Did he take advantage of you?"

She blanched. She felt her lips go numb with cold in spite of the sun. Gipsy must have been telling tales those times she'd gone over to the wharf to work on her tan. Joy had seen the two of them, dangling their feet in the water, laughing like conspirators. "We were just... friends. Brian has nothing to do with this," she said stiffly. It was true. If anybody had taught her the necessity of looking out for herself, it was her father, the man who'd drifted in and out of her life, shattered by loss, never there when she needed him.

She flung away the ice water and thrust the bucket at him. "Pumping the opposition's best friend—is that another one of your smart business moves?"

His rolling laugh went bounding down the hill. "Oho! Gipsy Connors doesn't need pumping for anything. She's all woman—generous, open, giving..."

She was stung by jealousy. Obviously Rain felt himself as free as the wind. And Gipsy could no more hold a conversation with a man without flirting than she could stop being beautiful. "Of course, that's what every red-blooded man dreams of, a woman who'll give him everything he wants. At every opportunity."

His hand closed on her arm and he pulled her roughly toward him, so that she felt his taut, hard male outline, heard the fast menacing rhythm of his breathing. "The playboy philosophy—is that what you think my creed is? I should've known it was too much to hope for—

that you'd take the trouble to know the real Rain MacCallum."

She met his gaze as long as she could. The hostility she saw there blurred everything else: his face, the sun, the crickets. Her knees started shaking and she dropped her eyes in confusion. Abruptly he let go of her arm. She stumbled and made for the car. By the time he followed with the picnic things, the storm had cleared.

"By the way," he said smoothly, as she backed onto the grass. "You never asked me what I thought the solution should be."

She frowned; she'd forgotten. Sell him the cottage, what else?

"Don't you want to hear it?"

"No! I don't!" She pushed her foot to the floor.

"Okay! Okay!" He laughed and put a big brown hand on the dashboard to steady himself as the Honda hit the gravel road. "It'll keep. If things get bad enough at the café, you know where to find me."

She bit her lip and was silent. At that moment, she hated him almost as passionately as she loved him.

CHAPTER EIGHT

FROM THE DESK IN HER OFFICE, Joy was able to look straight through the dining room bow window at Rain stringing Chinese lanterns on the rear deck of La Grosse Grenouille.

Pretty, the soft oranges and greens of the pleated paper globes in the noon sun; as for Rain—she swallowed. It was three days since that unfortunate picnic at Auberge des Vents and they hadn't exchanged a word. Should she go over now, while he was alone, and try again to explain about relocating the houseboat? she wondered, for what had to be the tenth time. Would he listen? For the tenth time her face flushed and she rejected the idea. Grimly, she bent over accounts payable.

It was difficult to concentrate with Gipsy chattering in the next room. Their only diner was a balding, bespectacled little man from the Chamber of Commerce doggedly eating zucchini quiche. Gipsy leaned against the table as though he were a long-lost friend. The times Joy had told her not to...

She put the dairy invoice on top of the something-on-account pile and sauntered into the dining room to catch Gipsy's eye. "Perhaps Monsieur Dépinard would like his tea *now*?" she emphasized.

"Sure! No problem," trilled Gipsy, starting for the kitchen.

Joy winced. "And could I see you in the office a few minutes, before you leave work this afternoon?"

She was moodily watching Rain shift big wooden tubs of chrysanthemums around as easily as if they were cookie canisters, when Gipsy dropped into the chair opposite the desk with a swirl of sky-blue skirts.

"Changed your mind about going to the party tonight?"

Joy gave a start. "Certainly not." She moved the dairy invoice to the bottom of the pile. The butcher was more likely to cut her off if her payment was late.

"I think you're making a big mistake. The boat's bound to be swarming with the most gorgeous females."

"I don't want to talk about it. And speaking of mistakes, how many times have I asked you not to lean on the tables? And not to be so familiar with the customers?"

"Aw, the little guy looked lonesome." Gipsy stretched her arms luxuriously over her lovely head. "I thought he'd enjoy a feminine wile or two."

"Monsieur Dépinard happens to have a wife and five children. He might enjoy silence even more."

"Come on, Joy! Don't be so stodgy. You're taking all the fun out of the café."

"The café *isn't fun*!" she snapped. "It's business. And difficult as it may be for you to believe, not all men want to be entertained by a one-woman floor show."

Gipsy stared at her with interest. "You've got it bad, haven't you? What are you holding out for? Relax—go to the party. He invited you, remember?"

"Yes—to make sure I don't raise the roof when the noise gets out of hand. Of course he did." She ran a distracted hand through her curls and grimaced. "I'm beginning to sound like what's-her-name. That bad-tempered witch in the comic strips. Worse, I even feel like her. You're going to the party, I take it?''

"Would you hold it against me?''

"You spend half your time over there anyway.'' *Fraternizing with the enemy* she'd almost said—not only bad-tempered, but jealous and petty as well. She was finding out all kinds of truths about herself. Darn Rain MacCallum anyway.

Gipsy pouted. "I've got to do something. The café's not very busy. Waiting on old geezers and cleaning salt and pepper shakers doesn't exactly take my mind off Bruno.''

Guilt made her feel worse. "I warned you. You said you wanted peace and quiet.''

"I know. But day after day of the stuff? Somehow I thought Bruno would have tracked me down by now. Not a single phone call...'' Her sigh spoke volumes. Joy felt too depressed to answer. Now both of them were staring moodily at the houseboat. One of the workmen had arrived; he and Rain were stringing fairy lights from the railed observation deck to the tops of the masts.

"Yves. Isn't that his name? Kind of cute with that curly black hair. I wonder if he'll be there tonight?''

It was Joy's turn to sigh. Gipsy would be all right, Bruno or no Bruno; she was a survivor. "Any idea what you're going to wear?''

Gipsy came alive. "I've been meaning to ask. That little boutique off rue L'Église has the most divine creation in the window. Okay with you if I borrow the Honda and drive into town?''

Joy produced the car keys from her straw handbag. "Go ahead.''

"Come with me. Buy something new yourself and knock Rain dead, why don't you?"

"I'm not going tonight. Remember?" She reached for her checkbook and envelopes. The shape her finances were in, she couldn't have bought a new pair of stockings.

"If it's money—" Gipsy paused in the doorway. "I've got a bit put aside."

Joy waved her off without looking up, so the sudden tears in her eyes wouldn't show. "How can I get these bills paid if you keep hanging around? Show me the dress when you get back."

BY JOY'S STANDARDS, it was outrageously flamboyant and recklessly extravagant. On Gipsy, it looked absolutely stunning. Shimmering emerald green with a svelte halter top, the dress had a hip-hugging skirt that ended in a fluted tumble of pleats. She had taken the curling iron to the tendrils hanging about her neck and temples, and added silver hoop earrings. Joy cast an admiring glance at her friend's image in the mirror. "Spanish Gipsy tonight. Talk about knocking them dead!"

Gipsy struck a flamenco pose, then clasped Joy's hands impulsively in hers. "You could still change your mind. Wear that designer sundress of mine..."

The skirt alone had four yards of material in it and the dress was patterned all over with enormous cabbage roses. The picture of Joy wearing it was so ridiculous, both girls burst out laughing.

"Stop worrying about me. I've got a letter to write to my father—one I've put off much too long already. After that it's early to bed."

She was tired enough, she told herself; the dining room had been full of people who'd counted on a cruise and found La Grosse Grenouille booked for a party. A phone call had brought Madame Hebert, almost cheerful in a pair of Adidas a daughter had bought for her. They'd improvised shamelessly, adding stuffed cucumbers and eggs Florentine to the buffet and even, after discovering a jar of artichoke hearts at the back of the shelf, a salad Joy dubbed the ButterCup. She had waited on tables herself so Gipsy could take her time dressing. Now she saw her off across the road and watched the brilliant emerald merge with the colorful dresses already on board. A live band was warming up on the rear deck, and the Chinese lanterns were starting to glow as the last crimson streamers of sunset faded behind the mountains.

Resolutely she shut and bolted the front door against the sight of Rain, resplendent in white trousers and a midnight-blue shirt open at the neck, welcoming his female guests with a kiss on both cheeks, French fashion. JS was outside somewhere. She called once or twice from the back door but there was no response—maybe he was having better luck with his Saturday nights than she was.

She took a brisk shower and climbed into bed with her notepad. Rain's comment about porcupine quills was still festering, and this morning she had hunted up her father's last address. She had never told him about the café. Over the years, she hadn't told him about a lot of things. It was easier that way, less painful. But lately, she had begun to see her father differently—as a man first and a father second. The old childhood sense of disappointment and resentment was fading. In its place, she was aware of a dawning compassion for the man whose grief had left him incapable of responding to her own. Was it too late, she wondered, to let him know?

The letter started off well, but halfway down the page she ran out of steam. She turned and punched the pillows. The band was turning out to be harder to ignore than she'd expected. It was a classy combination of guitar, drums and flute. Sounds were magnified by the water; there had to be at least forty voices out there, all chattering and laughing, but she could still pick out Rain's, and every time she did, something hurt inside her head. Maybe she should have driven to Sainte Agathe for the evening to watch a movie instead. Somebody had strayed across the road and was hammering on her front door. Irritably she chewed on her pen; it wasn't her fault if they couldn't read the Closed sign. Whoever it was gave up. She wrote another laborious sentence and sat bolt upright. Footsteps were thudding up her stairs. She'd left the back door unlocked for Gipsy. She reached for her dressing gown as the door burst open. She froze.

"You!"

Rain looked every inch of his six foot two, and even more devastatingly handsome close up. Also furious. "What the hell are you doing here?" he rasped.

She dropped the gown and yanked the duvet higher. "Me! What are *you* doing here?"

"Gipsy told me you'd be in bed. I thought she was kidding. Of all the crazy—" He paused, eyes narrowing. "Or is it? I suppose you're actually going to try and sleep. At nine forty-five! So tomorrow you can wail about how I kept you awake for hours."

It had crossed her mind—serve him right. "I never wail," she said coldly. "I'm writing to my father, if you must know."

"On a Saturday night, with the biggest bash of the year going on across the road? I suppose it slipped your mind that you were invited?"

"That wasn't an invitation. You just wanted to make sure you're covered for when the party lasts until 4:00 a.m. and shatters the sound barrier."

"See? See what I'm up against?" He moved closer to the bed. She caught a whiff of Aramis—no wood shavings tonight. The white slacks taut over his muscular thighs were the latest style. A gold chain glinted at his neck and the blue V of his shirt framing a dusting of curly russet hair was pure silk. When he caught her eye, something like electricity flashed between them. "Do you always have to be so unrelentingly *smug* about assuming the worst? Damn it, Joy, I'm not asking now. I'm ordering you to come!"

She sat up, forgetting the duvet. "Ordering? The café's on the brink of bankruptcy, thanks to you, and you have the nerve to break in here and start *ordering*? Wild horses wouldn't drag me to your party. *So get out!*" She couldn't believe the voice was hers. She hadn't yelled like that since she was twelve. He looked taken aback, but only for a second.

"Listen, Miss High-and-Mighty. You don't need wild horses. I'll carry you over there myself." He stood towering over her. The entire room vibrated with his presence, unabashedly male and charged with anger. She shrank against the pillows.

"You lay a finger on me and I—I'll call the police."

A mocking amusement crept into his expression. "Go ahead. I'm all ears."

Both telephones were downstairs; she should have known he'd call her bluff. "I'll scream," she threatened.

"Scream away," he said comfortably. The band had just launched into an old Creedence Clearwater Revival number. Maybe he'd even selected the songs for their decibel count before he came up. "Five minutes," he announced, "that's what I'm giving you to get out of bed and into some clothes."

"You're crazy. You can't make me—"

"Can't I?" He leaned down and whipped the duvet off the bed, exposing her full length in the old sleeveless shirt she wore when it was really hot and she wanted comfort, not concealment. She shrieked, grabbing at the dressing gown which had slid to the floor. He snatched it away and held it up, teasing.

"You want to wear this to the party instead? Or how about what you've got on right now? Fetching!"

She swung her legs over the side of the bed. She trembled with rage and the strange aroused excitement he always managed to generate in her. "You'll pay for this, Rain."

He chuckled. "For what? I haven't laid a finger on you. Yet," he added softly.

She countered by switching off the bedside lamp, not that it made an appreciable difference. She'd forgotten about the moon and the glow from across the road. She hugged a pillow to her middle, disturbingly aware that there was nothing she'd like better than to feel his touch—but she'd die rather than let him know. She tossed her head. "There's a name for what you're doing," she said. "It's called sexual harassment and there's a law against it."

"Is that so?" He dropped the dressing gown on a flowered chintz chair, just out of reach. For a long pregnant moment he looked at her, eyes hooded so that only the gleam of his pupils showed. "You're mis-

taken, you know. This is nothing like sexual harassment. This is something much more old-fashioned
called seduction. And if I remember rightly, it was a
highly pleasurable game, that two could play.''

Her heart was beating so fast, she couldn't breathe.
She felt sure her face was crimson. ''I—I don't have a
dress to wear,'' she whispered. ''I wasn't coming, remember?''

He clutched his hands to his head. ''God give me pa-
tience,'' he muttered, turning to the closet. ''What
about this one? No. This one.'' He tossed it onto the
bed. It was a sleeveless white linen sheath she hadn't
worn in ages.

''I thought you wanted glamour.''

He gave her a pitying look. ''Glamour's the woman,
not the dress. Do I have to dig out what goes under-
neath, too?''

''No!'' Hastily she crossed to the dresser and pulled
what she needed out of the drawer. Her limbs were all
silvery in the light. The hem of her shirt flounced
against the back of her thighs and she could feel his eyes
on her. ''The bathroom?'' she queried, gaze downcast.

''Right,'' he said, clearing his throat. ''Four minutes, forty seconds, now.''

''You can't mean it,'' she gasped, scooping high-
heeled white sandals out of the closet on her way.

He shrugged. ''I can always help.'' She fled into the
bathroom and bolted the door.

She made it in four minutes and thirty-eight seconds, and that included lipstick, violet eyeshadow and
a misting of Quelques Fleurs. High-handed, domineer-
ing—she'd show him! If she was going to be forced to
do this, she'd do it right. He was lounging in the balcony door, contemplating the scene across the road,

when she came out. For an instant the bearded masculine profile, the tilted breadth of his shoulders contrasted with his narrow hips, made her knees go weak. She caught herself crisply. "Coming?"

Startled, he swung around. His eyebrows climbed, his mouth opened.

She did the model's pirouette she had learned from Gipsy, patted her curls and threw him the smile that showed her dimples.

"Joy..." he breathed. She didn't wait but started down the stairs. He caught up with her in the foyer. "You're lovely," he said. "Even lovelier than I expected."

"Really," she said sweetly, locking the door behind them. The tang of pine wafted down the hill on the night air. They picked their way among the parked cars. Gone was the hulking frog outline of the boat. Twinkling, glowing strings of light transformed it into a mysterious, airy palace floating on a trembling bed of color. Moonlight wavered in a path across the lake to where the mountains loomed black and secret under the night sky.

"Kubla Khan would have loved it," Joy whispered. Then, breaking the spell, she asked, "Where's Grabber?"

"With one of my men in Lac Désir." He sounded defensive.

"Just asking." At least JS wouldn't be subject to any unpleasant surprises, wherever he was.

The beat of the music quickened and Joy's heels tapped an accompaniment on the wharf. Flowers spilled out of tubs and windowboxes everywhere; Rain hadn't missed a trick. "Great band," she said. "I can hardly wait to start dancing." She felt his puzzled glance even before he spoke.

"Did I miss something back there?"

"Like what?" she enquired innocently.

"Like what brought about this sudden change of heart. Let me rephrase that. What is it that makes a woman so damn difficult for a man to understand?"

"We're not difficult." She slipped a hand under his arm crossing the gangplank. "Just different. Men got all the brawn and women have to make do with what's left." She waved gaily at the first familiar face she saw amid the hubbub on the deck. "Clémence! Nice to see you!"

A sleek younger man in a navy blazer sprang forward to help her on deck. Clémence, wand slim in silver lamé with sequins sparkling in her hair, made the introductions.

"Paul Gerard. Anything you need in diesel engines, Paul's the man." Leaning close to Joy, she said, "*Dieu merci*, you came. He's much too young for me. Where did you get that dress? You look *ravissante*. Do you not agree, Paul, she looks *ravissante*?"

He did, throwing in several other complimentary terms for good measure. Slipping a hand under Joy's elbow, he guided her into the lounge, where the bar was doing a thriving business. A glance over her shoulder showed Rain, his progress blocked by a portly man in a Hawaiian shirt, staring after her uneasily.

"A glass of white wine? Punch? Tell me your wish."

"A Dubonnet, please. With plenty of ice."

Paul Gerard relayed their orders to the bartender. The catering van from Sainte Agathe had been back and forth all afternoon; Rain was sparing no expense. The big handsome room was at its best, alive with stylish people. Evidently Rain had started the evening by giving his guests a tour of La Grosse Grenouille. Enthusiastic conversation about houseboats competed in two languages with the music drifting in from the deck. An attractive young woman with a cloud of dark hair, wearing an ankle-length gown that echoed the orange of Rain's regatta painting, was telling a man in a yachting cap that she simply had to have a houseboat for her birthday. Paul moved closer as he handed Joy her glass.

"So, tell me about yourself. Trust Rain MacCallum to know how to pick them! Close friends, are you?"

Joy felt her cheeks redden. "Actually, I'm a neighbor. I own the café across the road."

"Ah. *La charmante* ButterCup. I will make a point of dropping in for lunch."

"Do," she said, but without much warmth. He wasn't a type she cared for; too suave, too sure of himself, with his stocky blond good looks and his eyes all over her. Too pushy, she thought, as he slid a hand around her waist and said, "What do you say we go out on deck? Find a quiet corner to ourselves. Maybe you can give a hungry bachelor a few recipes."

Through the crowd she glimpsed Rain, working his way toward them, a determined set to his jaw. "Why not," she said, resisting an urge to shake off Paul Gerard's hand. They stood at the rail in a patch of shadow behind the platform Rain had erected for the band, while he told her about the big sale he'd made to an American boat manufacturer.

"I'm good at what I do. The best," he said, putting his glass down and leaning both hands on the rail with her pinned in between. "But you don't just want to hear about diesel engines. Pretty girl like you. Tell me, what do you do with your time off?"

"Weed the garden." Joy laughed, but it was the truth.

"Come on. *Sérieusement.*" He leaned closer. "Something that turns you on..."

Gipsy's lilting laugh rang across the deck. *Saved*, thought Joy, catching a flash of emerald skirt near the buffet. "Turns me on?" She swallowed the last of her Dubonnet. "Right now," she said brightly, "that would be food. Do you think Rain has lobster?"

The buffet had been set up on trestle tables under the awning. People milled and clustered. "Joy darling! You changed your mind!" Gipsy's pleasure at seeing her was reassuring. "Who's the Prince Charming?"

"Gipsy, Paul Gerard. Paul, my good friend Gipsy Connors." Her eyes telegraphed an appeal which Gipsy fielded neatly. "Paul, *enchantée*! You're here for the food, of course. Take my place in line—no, I absolutely insist! Joy, there are some people at my table who'd love to meet you." Effortlessly, she drew Joy into her circle. Being Gipsy, the circle was entirely male and high profile.

"The ButterCup—you don't say! Some friends of mine had the most delicious supper there last month. Dance, Miss Lowry?"

Two tables away Rain, once again detained in conversation, scowled. "I'd love to," she said with a smile.

He was somebody high up in banking, with silver hair and eyes to match, in striking contrast to a tan Joy guessed was year-round.

"Quite a guy, Rain MacCallum. But I'm sure I don't have to tell you that." He flashed a smile as he waltzed her onto the deck. "He's got some big plans. Very big."

"Really," she murmured.

"He'll pull them off, too. He's got the drive, the know-how. And the houseboat's a commodity whose time has come. This is one project the bank had no qualms approving."

Maybe she should have opened a floating diner. It would have been nice to hear words even remotely similar from Monsieur Thierry. She waited until she saw Rain sit down with a couple of VIP-looking men and their bored-looking wives, before pleading hunger and making her way to the buffet. Mounds of tender pink shrimp vied with plump lobster claws and a delicate salmon mousse garnished with watercress—things the ButterCup couldn't begin to afford. She heard laughter punctuating the conversation at Gipsy's table and felt a twinge of guilt at the sight of Rain's handsome bearded face brooding across the room at her. Back at the buffet to sample some curly green fiddleheads flown in from the Maritimes and done in a wine marinade, she half expected the light step behind her. But instead of Rain, it was Paul. His eyes were bland.

"Finally got a chance to eat, did you?"

"Oh, Paul..."

"You won't refuse me a dance?"

"Well, I—"

He took the plate out of her hand and led her near the stage, where the band was doing lovely things with an old Edward Bear song. He was no good at dancing, she quickly realized; he'd simply wanted to get his arms around her. They'd circled the deck once, bumping into Clémence and the mayor, when Rain loomed out of nowhere and tapped Paul on the shoulder. Something in his face made the salesman step back immediately. Joy found herself roughly pulled into Rain's arms.

"What do you think you're doing?" he asked through clenched teeth. She couldn't see his face; he was holding her too tightly.

"Having a good time. Isn't that what you brought me over here for?"

"You know damn well what I mean. I haven't been able to get near you for an hour."

"Don't feel bad. A host has to mingle," she said, flippantly. "Think of all the houseboats you've been selling."

The muscles of his arms tensed. "I'm talking about you, damn it! Not me. Every time I get within hailing distance, you're off with somebody else. He isn't your type, Joy," he added succinctly.

"Paul, you mean?" She tilted her face. "Does that bother you?"

He swung her past the railing. An orange lantern ignited copper sparks in his hair. "Sure it bothers me. It bothers any decent guy when a nice girl gets taken in by a smooth-talking make-out artist."

"Aren't you forgetting something? I'm the one who wears porcupine quills."

He groaned. She felt his breath stir her hair. The lights of Lac Désir shimmered across the bay. It was Saturday night and people were having a good time. "Joy?" he said quietly, and his arms tightened again. "What you said earlier. About the café going bankrupt. Did you mean it?"

She closed her eyes. She didn't want to answer. She didn't want to set the whole train of accusation and defense and resentment in motion again. All she wanted was to give herself up to the moment. To the feel of his arms holding her in tenderness, not anger, and the thump of his heart keeping time with the guitar playing "Yesterday."

"Joy?"

When he said her name in that tone, she could have melted with love. But love was no good bottled up inside. It was only good if you gave it away. He stopped dancing and lifted her chin with a finger so he could look into her face. "Why didn't you tell me it was that bad?"

"I did. All those times you said I was complaining or on the defensive. I was telling you."

He shook his head. "Just like a woman. Needling and nagging. Instead of coming straight out with it."

"I've got my pride. Just like a man."

They stood there, arms at their sides, eyeing each other like opponents in a ring while the last chord drifted over the water. "Thanks," he said, "for the dance." She watched him cross the deck with his easy, careless stride. Now what was she supposed to do, run along home? If she did, it would mean he'd won. Instead she put on the smile that showed her dimples and went to join Clémence, who'd been waving from the big corner table.

"Join us, *ma petite*. Yves here is too bashful to say so, but I happen to know he is dying to dance with you."

She did her best to look as though she was enjoying herself. Paul Gerard was sitting by himself, nursing a scotch and soda; thank heaven he seemed to have given up the pursuit. Gipsy twirled by with a geranium in her hair, consoling herself for Bruno's absence by conducting a campaign to make every man on the boat fall madly in love with her. Joy wondered if it helped and smiled experimentally at Yves. Then she saw Rain again, and she knew it was a hopelessly silly idea.

He was checking the buffet, leaning across for a word with the caterer's man. When he turned, the woman with the cloud of dark hair bumped into him, holding a full glass of punch. Five minutes later, the damage repaired, the two of them were swaying cheek to cheek on the deck to something slow and dreamy. She was tall and willowy. Clémence frowned. "Watch out for that one. Her father owns the biggest marina in the Laurentians," she murmured. Bold as brass over his partner's shoulder, Rain threw Joy a wink.

It didn't help to tell herself that what she felt was an acute case of shoe-on-the-other-foot. Taking the coward's way out, she excused herself and went to find the bathroom. It was cedar paneled and smelled of Aramis; a jar of dried rushes flanked the mirror. Just for an instant she saw what Rain had seen: the white dress, a foil for warm brown arms, a petite hourglass figure and a halo of tousled gold ringlets. The image faded, and she saw only a woman whose lipstick had worn off and whose eyes had the bruised look of unshed tears. It was crazy to hang around feeling like this. She was going home.

Halfway down the passage, she heard footsteps on the stairs. People were wandering all over the boat; what if it was Rain, giving Miss Dark Hair a personal tour? She ducked around a corner and found herself on a deck she hadn't seen before. It was snug as a cave, with one side open to the lake. Moonlight revealed a deck chair and a table ingeniously fashioned from a tree stump. Photographs lay strewn over the polished top next to an open box, as though there hadn't been time to put them away. She bent to look. With a start she realized most of them were of the cottage, taken over a long span of years. One of them, dog-eared and faded, showed a smiling man and woman sitting on the front step with their arms around a young boy who was obviously Rain. She sank onto the arm of the chair, feeling sick.

"So, this is where you are hiding, *ma belle*." It was Paul Gerard; he looked around. "*Intime. Privé.* I like it."

Joy stood up. "I don't think we should be here." She cleared her throat. "This must be Rain—Mr. Mac-Callum's—private deck."

"So it would appear." He strolled forward into the light. "You're crying. It's MacCallum's fault, isn't it?"

"I don't think that's any of your business." She dashed a hand over her wet cheeks. "I'm all right."

"Are you? I've been watching you, Joy. You have not been very happy tonight, have you?"

His suave tone was mesmerizing. Mutely, she shook her head.

"I thought as much. To be happy, a woman needs a man she can turn to. Love—"

"I'm all right now, really," she said hastily. "If you'll just let me get by. I want to go home."

He caught hold of her arm. His grip was surprisingly strong. "What's your hurry? You are afraid of me?"

"Of course not! Let go of me, please." His breath smelled of scotch; his blue eyes were red rimmed. "Rain MacCallum is not the only fish in the sea," he said, slurring the words slightly. "Maybe you should give somebody else a chance—"

"You, for example?" Rain loomed in the entrance, face like a thundercloud. "You want to give Paul Gerard a chance, Joy?"

Paul's hand fell away and she started back guiltily. The contempt in Rain's voice took her breath away. "No," she gasped, as he stepped onto the deck.

"You heard the lady. Get out, Gerard. Party's over for you."

Paul's tone was jeering. "Dog in the manger, is that it, MacCallum? Making sure nobody else can have what you don't want."

"Why, you—" Menacingly, Rain started forward. "You're drunk!" he exclaimed in disgust. "Get out and stay out! From now on, peddle your engines someplace else. They're not worth the price of having you around."

Paul blanched and backed clumsily into the railing. He put out a hand to steady himself, encountered empty air and overbalanced.

"Hey!" Rain made a grab for him, but it was too late. Paul was already toppling backward over the railing. His yell of astonishment terminated abruptly in a resounding splash. Horrified, Joy rushed forward and peered into the water until she saw him surface, sputtering and thrashing. Heads appeared over the railing of the deck below. Somebody shouted instructions, a lifeline was thrown into the water, and hands were reaching out. When she turned, Rain had gone.

The passageway was empty. The music had stopped and a tide of excited voices, all talking at once, rose from below. Joy gave a little involuntary moan. She spied a ladder to the ceiling and pulling off her sandals, clambered up the rungs. She thrust aside the trapdoor at the top and came out, as she had expected, on the observation deck.

She straightened and looked down, blessedly far above the commotion below. Paul was being hauled, swearing, on deck. Everyone trailed indoors, asking questions. No way was she going down there to face them. She'd felt mortified enough in front of Rain—especially in front of Rain! She sank limply onto the bench that ran around the rim of the deck. So much for her brave show of independence. On shore the cottage glowed like a lantern against the dark backdrop of pines. She'd forgotten to turn off the light in the bedroom. "Dog in the manger," that dreadful Paul Gerard had said: Rain making sure nobody else got what he didn't want. She couldn't believe that. Rain did want her... didn't he?

She threw back her head and stared at the stars in the clear northern sky. She picked out Orion's Belt, and the Big and Little Dippers—one of the few things she'd learned from her father. A cooling breeze fanned her cheeks. The scent of wild raspberries, sharp and sweet, mingled with the dark, weedy smell of water. Voices called out from the gangplank, *"Bonsoir, Rain! Merci millefois!"* She watched the headlights of the cars swing into the road. Only midnight; the party was breaking up early. Her fault, she supposed. He'd probably accuse her of engineering the whole thing.

When Rain poked his head through the trapdoor a few minutes later, she didn't say a word.

Neither did he, at first. He stood in the center of the deck, with his hands making fists in the pockets of his white slacks, and stared at the caterer's van spinning its tires in the sand.

"Hole like a moon crater. I told him, park at the café." He turned. His tone was matter-of-fact. "I thought you'd be up here. I told Gipsy not to worry. Just to go to bed."

"Thanks. Is—was Paul Gerard all right?"

"Seemed to be. Emptied my Napoléon brandy, borrowed my best suit and assured Gipsy she had Spanish eyes."

She smiled faintly. "I didn't even *like* him." She looked up to meet his eyes. "Oh, Rain, I'm sorry."

"What for? You don't have to apologize to me. What you do, and who you do it with, is your business."

She felt her color rise. "It wasn't what you think. I stumbled on your little deck, well, by mistake. He must have followed me."

"Sure. The way he followed you all evening."

She sat up very straight. She could have mentioned Miss Dark Hair, or the photographs, but she felt it was beneath her. "I didn't ask to come here tonight. And you do business with Paul. You should know what he's like."

"Right. Rub it in." He shrugged a blue silk shoulder. "Let's just forget it happened, shall we?" He looked tired, his hair dishevelled, and his mind obviously on other things. "Let's talk about us instead. Now that you've had a chance to see MacCallum Houseboats from this side of the road, what do you think?"

She moved restlessly on the bench. "If that's what you brought me over here to ask—"

"Wait, it's important. I don't want any doubts in your mind about my ability to succeed."

She stood up, her face anguished. "I've already told you, I'm glad for you. What else do you want from me?"

"Joy, please. I've put a lot of thought into this." He placed big firm hands on her shoulders and looked into her eyes, so that her heart moved painfully in her breast.

"I want you to make me a partner in the ButterCup Café."

She stared at him. She had to be more tired than she thought. "Are you serious?"

"Don't look like that. Sure, I'm serious. We'll hammer out terms with a lawyer, sign an agreement. All strictly business."

Strictly business—the phrase reverberated. Not because he cared. "I don't understand, Rain. Why would you want to? I told you what financial shape the ButterCup's in."

He waved a hand in dismissal. "Naturally, as a partner I'd invest money, a cash infusion. I figure we'd be able to combine operations—the café and the cruises. Coordinate schedules, share clients. You could be in charge of purchasing and food preparation. God knows, I need help with this business of providing food day to day, now that construction is shifting into high gear."

"How nice for you! You'd take over, in other words. I'd be working for you." All her pride, her sense of accomplishment, rose in protest. "Me, the café, everything I've built up on my own—"

"Partner, I said." He looked at her in irritation. "I'd be your partner. Not your boss. Of course I'd expect your cooperation in return."

"Oh, of course. Partner—cooperation—that's a laugh! We can't even get on as neighbors."

"Well, if that's your attitude—"

"Be realistic, Rain!" She was dismayed to hear a note of pleading creep into her voice. "We don't even want the same things. There's too much inequality between us for partnership. Too many points of contention." She forced herself to meet his gaze squarely. "The cottage, for instance, would you want a share in that, too?''

He looked uncomfortable. ''The cottage *is* the café. So I suppose...'' His brows drew together. ''Listen, this is a commonsense solution to a couple of mutual problems. Let's leave suspicion and emotion out of it.''

But they were in it already. She was in love with him, and he— She dropped her eyes. All she could see were the photographs, spread across the tree-stump table in the moonlight. She'd only be laying herself open to more heartache and aggravation. ''I . . . I'll think about it,'' she said. ''But the way I feel now, I'd prefer to take my chances with Monsieur Thierry.''

He drew in his breath. ''Right,'' he said. Brusquely he turned, unplugged something and the lights winked off all over the boat. ''I thought you'd jump at the chance. But I guess I was wrong. Shall we go?''

''Rain?'' At the top of the ladder she touched his hand. ''Are you angry?''

''Angry! Is that what you think?''

Something flickered in his eyes and he ran his fingers lightly down the side of her cheek. ''Know something?'' He slid an arm around her waist and dropped a kiss on her reluctant lips.

''What?'' she whispered.

''We'd have made a great team.''

Past tense. She felt chilled. ''Would we?''

The corner of his mouth curved upward under his mustache in a lopsided grin. ''Can you doubt it?''

He kissed the tip of her nose, then her right earlobe. His hand brushed possessively over the front of her dress. Her eyes widened in protest and he kissed them shut. He nuzzled her hair. ''Mmm,'' he said and pulled her closer. He wrapped long arms around her, moulded her to him. With a shock she felt the strength of his arousal and the leap of an answering flame in her veins. She struggled to free herself. This wasn't what she wanted, not when everything else between them was wrong. His grip tightened; he tilted her head back roughly and kissed her again, his tongue forcing her lips apart with hot driving intensity.

He thrust her backward onto the bench, pinning her down with the weight of his body. She gasped as the wooden edge dug into her spine. His kiss burned deeper, exploring, claiming her. There was no playfulness now, no gentleness, only the hard wanting of his hands over her body, the ragged sound of his breathing. She felt him unfasten the zipper at the back of her dress and work the fabric down over her shoulders, and her body went rigid. *Oh Rain,* she thought in a kind of despair, as his hand slid under the lace of her slip, *not here, like this.* His palm moved, rough and warm, over the tender swell of her breast and against her will she felt herself melting, melting, holding her breath to keep from crying out. Then, suddenly, he withdrew his hand and lay still.

She felt his mouth leave hers, saw him raise his head, blocking out the stars wheeling far above them. "Rain?" she whispered.

His breathing slowed. Heavy-eyed, sombre, he gazed down at her.

"It's no good like this, is it?" he said quietly.

CHAPTER NINE

JOY TURNED UP the kitchen radio, in the faint hope that Mozart would drown out the rock and roll pounding through the ceiling. All it did was make her headache worse.

She pushed aside her recipe file and poured herself another coffee, black. For the first time in her life she didn't feel like cooking. In quick succession Rain had taken her heart, then her customers, now her will to cook. Maybe even her will to live, she reflected wryly. The ceiling went silent and Gipsy came bounding down the stairs in time to a cheerful off-key whistling. She stopped at the sight of Joy, hunched over the kitchen table in her yellow ButterCup sweatshirt, staring at a blank menu sheet.

"Well! Good morning! What time did *you* get in last night? Not that it's any of my business."

"No," agreed Joy without looking up. "It isn't."

"Ah!" Gipsy reached for the coffeepot. "What happened? Are you going to tell me or are you going to let me fantasize?"

"Nothing happened," said Joy irritably, switching off Mozart and moving her menu sheets out of harm's way as Gipsy descended on the table with a brimming mug.

"Nothing? In a setting out of *The Arabian Nights*? With a one-hundred-percent male like Rain Mac-

Callum playing the lead? Joy, darling, you can do better than that."

It was no good; she never could hide anything from Gipsy. She felt a telltale blush mantling her cheeks. "Well, almost nothing happened." Certainly by Gipsy's standards, almost nothing.

"That's not what your face is saying." Gipsy rolled her eyes ceilingward. "Why, oh why, is it always the angelic-looking blondes?" She helped herself to a fresh blueberry muffin and slathered it with butter. "That kind of 'nothing' should happen to me! 'Handsome hero knocks oily villain into lake for daring to lay hands on heroine.'"

Joy gave a gasp. "Did Rain tell you that?"

"Rain, typical male, didn't say a word. I put two and two together."

"It was all a misunderstanding. Besides, Paul fell in by himself—Rain didn't push him. Gipsy, could we leave this subject? It's a lot more complicated than it seems. If I ever get it sorted out in my own head, you'll be the first to know."

"Okay."

Joy looked at her friend across the table. Honey-gold skin bared provocatively under her orange silk wrapper, black hair tumbling luxuriously over her shoulders, eyes dewy as moss after a spring shower. "You're cheerful this morning."

Gipsy arched her brow. "There's something about a party. Makes a girl feel good to know she's still in demand."

"Mm. What time did *you* get to bed last night?"

"Just after midnight. *And* alone." She sighed and reached for another muffin. "Bruno may not deserve it but he doesn't have a thing to worry about."

Joy returned to the recipe file. It was nine-thirty and the café opened for brunch at eleven. Aside from the muffins she hadn't prepared anything. Gipsy poured herself more coffee. "Rain made me an offer last night," she said.

Joy's stomach plunged through a trapdoor. She stared.

"Not that kind of offer!" exclaimed Gipsy. "Promise not to be mad?"

"Why should I be mad?" Cautiously she reassembled her stomach.

"You could look at it the wrong way. As though I were going over to the enemy."

"Gipsy, what are you talking about?"

"Rain wants me to work for him on the houseboat. As a kind of hostess and general girl Friday."

Relief was quickly succeeded by disbelief, and disbelief by anger. "You mean—he meant it, all this time he's been after you to be his social director?"

"Well, not at first. It started out as a joke. But then we got talking. I'd be an asset, he said. Aside from wages, I'd get tips. He was awfully persuasive."

"Oh, I can imagine. Persuasive Rain MacCallum."

"You *are* mad at me! Be reasonable, Joy. You really don't have enough work here for me. And the poor man needs help with those crowds. Besides," she flashed Joy a grin. "If I lean on tables and talk too much, it won't be a crime on the Bullfrog."

Betrayal wasn't too strong a word for it. "I thought you were my friend."

"I am. That doesn't change the fact that I could use the money. Models don't get paid when they don't work. My tips at the café didn't even pay for the dress I bought."

And whose fault was that? Moodily she watched Gipsy bite into her third muffin. If they were talking dollars and cents, she'd probably save a week's profits on her meals alone. But that wasn't the point.

"When does he want you to start?"

"This morning. I thought I'd wait awhile." She gave a shrug of laughter. "Give him a chance to get last night's glasses washed up first."

If she were Gipsy, thought Joy, she'd be over there right now, washing them for him. That was what love did to women. If she had agreed to a partnership with Rain, that was what she'd be doing in any case. Maybe if he'd held her and kissed her the way he did, before he asked instead of after, she would have decided differently. Thank God he didn't, and she hadn't, if this was the kind of duplicity he was capable of. She snapped the file shut and picked up the blank menu sheets. She could always leave out the Closed sign. Preparing Sunday brunch for the five or six people who might show up was a sure way to lose money. She stood up, smoothing her sweatshirt down over the hips of her neat cotton shorts.

"If you're not leaving until later," she said coolly, "maybe you could put the breakfast dishes in the dishwasher. I've got some—work to do outside."

Gipsy frowned. "I don't like that look in your eye. You're not thinking of going over there to give him a piece of your mind, are you?"

"Fat lot of good that would do, if you've already accepted." Besides, she knew where complaining got her with Rain; needling and nagging he called it. "I'm going to do something I should have done weeks ago." She let herself smartly out the screen door, before Gipsy could ask.

There was a big commotion in the lilacs. JS dropped to the lawn at her feet in a flurry of leaves, pursued by the robin couple shrieking abuse. All week he'd been trying to sneak a look into their nest. "Get him!" she yelled at the birds, startling herself. Add ruthlessness to the traits Rain brought out in her; well, this time he would have to suffer the consequences himself.

He'd left the garage door wide open as usual, with a couple of truck tires propped against it. She moved purposefully around them into the dim interior. It smelled of musty wood, engine oil, turpentine—heaven only knew what else. Of course he hadn't picked up so much as a nail since their argument in the Supermarché. He'd added considerably, though, to the stuff already there: a roll of copper wiring nested in her wheelbarrow, some leaky paint cans had joined her preserving jars on the shelf, a sheet of plywood leaned against the handle of the lawnmower. Everything on her side, naturally, because his was already packed to the rafters.

All the better, she reasoned, pitching the copper wiring into the driveway; he'd have no comeback now, when she evicted him. Unfortunately her aim was off and the coil snaked through the air and decapitated one of the tomato plants. Angrily, she snatched at the paint cans, stubbed her toe on a chainsaw lurking half under the Honda's back bumper, and tumbled into a roll of metal sheeting. The clatter was unholy; worse, it went on and on as she struggled to get back on her feet. In a temper, she heaved the paint cans out the door and made a grab for the saw.

"Joy, no! Wait!"

The saw was heavier than she'd anticipated. She straightened up as the shout penetrated her consciousness. Rain was pelting across the road in nothing but his cut-off jeans and tan.

"Not my chainsaw! Woman, have you gone berserk? That saw cost hundreds!"

Out of the corner of her eye she saw Gipsy on the back step, her hand frozen over her mouth. Rain arrived, broad chest heaving. "Thank God, I'm in time!" He pried the saw from her grasp. "What got into you?"

Joy found her voice. "Into *me*?" she sputtered.

"I'll just put this safely over here," he went on soothingly, eyes searching his side of the garage for an open space. "Where nothing can happen to it."

"Not over there! I want everything out. Your lease is canceled. Terminated. As of this morning."

"Why?" He turned, frowning. "What did I do this morning?"

"You have the nerve to ask? After hiring Gipsy to work for you? As my competition?"

He had the grace to turn pale under the tan. He must have come over out of a sound sleep. His hair was disheveled and his eyes badly needed a splash of cold water. The jeans lacked a belt and hadn't quite made it over his narrow hips. "Hey, be fair! I asked her last night. Before I knew you were going to turn down the partnership idea."

"I get it." Furiously she tore her eyes away from the line of fine dark hair disappearing under his waistband. "It was going to be one big happy family. Where you could grab whatever you needed. My garage, my best friend—" Her voice broke. "Oh Rain, how could you?"

His shoulders stiffened. "Gipsy didn't see anything wrong with the idea. Under the circumstances."

"You were that sure of me?"

"Why not? What the hell do you think I was offering last night? I thought it was mutual assistance. Well, pardon me, I won't make that mistake again." He turned, deposited the saw on the driveway, and came back for the plywood.

"Excuse me," he said curtly, so that she was forced to move aside. She wished she wouldn't keep noticing how the muscles rippled under his bronze skin, or how his big graceful frame radiated dignity despite the lack of attire. She clasped her hands tightly and said, "I suppose you think you can't lose. Now you've got Gipsy, it's just a matter of time before I come around. Or give up the café."

He swept her a glance in which the ice was an inch thick. If she hadn't jumped out of the way, he would have trundled the tires over her foot. It was hard to believe this was the man who'd kissed her under the stars last night, whose touch had made her want to cry out for joy. If he'd said one tender word, or even smiled, she would have told him to forget the argument about Gipsy and leave his things where they were. But he didn't, and the suggestion died in her throat. Stiff with misery she made her way to the cottage and let herself in the back door. Gipsy had disappeared; the dishes hadn't been touched. Like a robot, she began loading them into the dishwasher.

The sounds from the driveway continued. She stored away the muffins and emptied the coffeepot, blanking out the knowledge that he probably hadn't had breakfast. It wasn't her fault the man needed a wife to look after him. To escape that thought, she went upstairs and thumped the duvet until it rose over the bed like a whipped meringue. When Rain backed his truck into the driveway and started tossing things into the back, she took a scrub brush to the bathroom, even though it didn't need scrubbing, and she polished the mirror until Monsieur Thierry's face glittered. After a time, with a clashing of gears, the truck drove away, squealing at the bend. She noticed it was awfully quiet in Gipsy's room.

The orange wrapper flopped across the unmade bed; Joy pushed the door open wider. Skirts and tops draped over the chair and abandoned on the floor testified to Gipsy's customary difficulty in deciding what to wear. Joy sighed, unplugged the curling iron, picked up a spilled bottle of Passion Plum nail polish, and shut the door on the rest.

She still had one friend that she knew of and on the third try, the line was free. Clémence had been on the phone, rounding up clients for a Sunday afternoon open house. She listened quietly before she broke in crisply with, "*Alors, ma petite.* Do not argue. Leave the Closed sign as it is and get yourself over here. You are having lunch with me today."

Joy hadn't the slightest desire to argue. It was heavenly to have someone with no ax to grind telling her what to do. She ran a hand over the dresses in her closet, determined to make the most of the occasion. Her self-respect needed all the help it could get. The weather was cooler today and she settled on a slim cream skirt with a slit up the back and a mocha blouse with a V-neck collar that ended in a softly draped bow. JS was annoyed when she locked him inside.

"For your own good," she told him. Those robins would stop at nothing.

The garage was not only empty, but swept as well. She felt as though she were driving a Rolls instead of a Honda when she backed into the drive without a single worry about nail punctures or squashed paint cans. Rain was sitting on his rear deck in the shade of the awning, chair tilted back and Adidas crossed in a box of petunias. She could feel his eyes on her as she swung into the road. He wasn't doing anything, not even reading. She couldn't recall ever having seen him like that before. She thought she saw Gipsy's head bobbing in the galley porthole, just about where the sink would be. Rain didn't wave, and Joy didn't either. She drove into Lac Désir feeling painfully disoriented, as though the world had turned upside down.

SUNLIGHT FILTERED through the lacy asparagus fern hanging in the bay window of Clémence's study. It illumined the tiny figures in flowing robes busy about their daily lives on the lacquered black Chinese screen. Restful, thought Joy, studying the little nineteenth century vignettes; not a houseboat or a café or a tall man in jeans among them. The screen was a beauty, the focal point of the room, and Clémence's big desk had been lacquered black to match. Everything else was ivory and white: the leather love seat on which Joy was sitting, the wool rug underfoot.

"*Voilà!* That did not take long, did it? So much cozier, I think, to finish our tête-à-tête in here." Clémence, looking smart and businesslike in a green silk shirtdress, set the coffee tray down on a glass table. "You like the screen? My late husband brought it back from a posting in Taiwan." She poured the steaming fragrant coffee into translucent silver-rimmed china cups and handed one to Joy. "Cream? Sugar?"

"I can't tell you how much I appreciate this." Joy leaned forward and helped herself. "The lovely lunch. The chance to talk."

They had eaten out-of-this-world salmon soufflé, just the two of them in grand style in Clémence's dining room, and Joy, encouraged by a glass of Momessin white, had poured out her tale of woe concerning the café, leaving out only the extent of her personal feelings toward Rain. Immediately, Clémence's nimble brain had started generating ideas.

"Bus tours!" she announced, taking her cup over to the desk. "Have you thought of approaching the people who run tours to the Laurentians? They're always on the lookout for scenic, not-too-dear restaurants."

"A busload is an awful lot," said Joy doubtfully. "Maybe if they have vans. Say a dozen people..." If she planned the menu right, and Madame Hebert brought Lisette to help... Her face brightened in spite of herself.

Clémence searched through a drawer. "I had it here somewhere. A cousin of mine works for Le Bel Horizon in Montréal. They specialize in tours for seniors... Here it is." She handed Joy a leaflet depicting a blue-and-white minibus charging a hill flaming with autumn foliage. She was already dialing. "I'll give him a call at home right now and introduce you. Maybe you can set up a meeting.... *Allô! Henri? Clémence ici. Ça va?*"

Henri sounded like a charming male edition of his cousin. He would be delighted to drive up next weekend, he said, and see for himself. "There's hope," marveled Joy, accepting more coffee. "At least I'll have something to tell Monsieur Thierry on Thursday."

Clémence lit a cigarette. "*Naturellement*, there is always the obvious course. Have you tried talking frankly to Rain MacCallum? Letting him know how things stand with the café? I recall as a boy he got into his

share of high-spirited scrapes, but he was never mean.
I cannot believe he is an unreasonable man.''

Joy stared unhappily into her cup. "We've talked.
We've tried to come to some kind of arrangement.'' The
partnership offer: on the surface, a generous gesture.
"But I can't trust him. I keep feeling he's after something. The cottage..."

"Maybe he is not sure of you, either."

"Me! What does he have not to be sure about?"

"Maybe he thinks—like you—that you are trying to
gain an advantage at his expense.'' The clear eyes were
shrewd. "Does he know you are in love with him?"

"I certainly hope not!" Joy reddened uncontrol-
lably; her heartbeat accelerated just thinking about it.
"He'd have me totally over a barrel if he knew. Besides, one thing has nothing to do with another."

"Do not be so sure." Clémence's expression softened. "The greatest gift in the world, love. And we are
so afraid of presenting it to one another."

Joy felt uncomfortable. "How did you know how I
feel about Rain? Is it so obvious?"

Clémence's beringed hand patted hers. "Only to
someone who has been there herself, as you so quaintly
say in English. The sun rose and set for me on Jean."

Jean LeClair had been a good deal older, somebody
with the Department of External Affairs, in Ottawa.
Clémence had dropped out of university and given up
a planned career in law to marry him. They'd had ten
blissful years together before he died and she came back
to Lac Désir to live. A classic love story it seemed to
Joy, from the bits and pieces she had heard. "Has there
never been anyone else?" she asked softly.

"Oh, several—they come and go, *n'importe!* But only one man so *merveilleux* I was willing to spend my life with him. Do you understand, *ma petite*?"

Joy nodded; she was starting to, whether she liked it or not.

"I still sometimes think with a shiver, if I had not chosen Jean, what I would have missed! And now..." She rose to her feet in a shimmer of pleats. "I am afraid it is time. The open house is at the old Quenneville place, on rue Principale. Do you know it? Come with me. Perhaps it will take your mind off your problems."

"The Quenneville place? I don't think so," said Joy, remembering the humiliating night Rain had sung its praises to her. "But thank you all the same."

At the door, Clémence held her at arm's length. "*Si jolie.* So young and full of courage. I do not see how Alphonse Thierry can say no." She smiled. "Wear what you are wearing now. He has a weakness for chic women."

SHE HOPED Clémence was right. It was Thursday afternoon and Joy's appointment with the bank was in half an hour. She was standing in front of the dresser mirror, fastening the clasp of her mother's pearls under Monsieur Thierry's stern eye. The light slanting through the balcony door was a dull gray; not a promising day for the Mont Tremblant boat show. "Rain's going, so I'll be in charge of the Bullfrog today," Gipsy had called over her shoulder on her way out earlier that morning. As if Joy cared! She had put on the cream skirt and mocha blouse again and done what she could with her face and hair. She looked chic enough, she supposed, but she didn't feel it.

It had not been a good week. Sunday's cooler weather had turned cloudy by evening, and on Monday it started to rain. It rained on and off for three days; people stayed home to eat, or if they were on vacation, they stayed in their hotels. On Tuesday, the waves were choppy and visibility was so poor that La Grosse Grenouille remained tied up at the wharf instead of cruising the lake. Standing disconsolately in the bow window after supper, Joy had watched the water drip off the awning pulled over the rear deck. The lake was the color of gun metal. Across the bay, Lac Désir lay hidden behind a curtain of rain. It hadn't seemed worth protesting when pop music pounded raucously across the road. A handful of people moved lethargically in and out of the blurred light of early dusk. Every now and then she'd caught sight of Gipsy in her swinging paisley skirt, carrying a tray of drinks, chattering to beat the band, sometimes dancing.

Of Rain, she had seen hardly anything since their mortifying encounter on Sunday. Half the time the truck was gone. Construction of the first houseboat had begun in Sainte Agathe, according to Madame Hebert. It was *"une arche de Noé"* she declared—a Noah's Ark rising bulkily from the sand and weedy grasses on the shore of Lac des Sables. Wednesday, when the clouds lightened for an hour or two, Joy had made the half-hour drive to the site, ostensibly to take a look for herself, but in reality drawn by a restless aching desire to see Rain.

He'd been directing the raising of the roof beam, and stood out like a Norse Viking amid the more slightly built French Canadian workmen. This was how she loved him best: larger than life, laughing and shouting encouragement to his men with that marvelous overflowing vitality of his. She hadn't dared linger; if he'd glanced up, he would have recognized the Honda. He'd arrived home in a shower that night, well after dark, sprinting down the wharf with his long, lithe stride and his yellow slicker thrown over his head. Joy remembered how Grabber had hurled himself at his master on the gangplank, and the two of them engaged in a wrestling match that nearly landed them both in the water. Peering between the slats of the blind, she'd wondered if Gipsy was making a bowl of hot soup for him in the shiny silver galley. Somehow she doubted it.

Lately she hadn't seen much of Gipsy, who often crept up to bed well after midnight. Mornings, she slept in, leaving while Joy was in the basement doing tablecloths, or at the market. Sometimes at six o'clock she dashed in to change. Politely, she would ask whether anyone had phoned for her; politely Joy would say no. It was a relief, in a way, not to have to find tasks to keep her occupied in the café.

Thursday morning, bank book in hand, Joy had calculated how best to divide her meager earnings. Madame Hebert hadn't worked this week, but the electricity bill was due, and she'd have to put money aside for groceries for the weekend, when the ButterCup was most likely to attract diners. She rubbed distracted ink-smudged fingers over her forehead. It left precious little for Monsieur Thierry.

Enough to appease him, she hoped anew, catching his disapproving stare from the picture on her office wall as she got her purse. His real-life expression across the bank's immaculate oak desk fifteen minutes later was remarkably similar. "Two hundred? *C'est tout?* Nothing personal, Mademoiselle Lowry, but the bank does not regard you as a good risk."

She clasped and unclasped her hands in her lap. "How can you say that? I've met all my payments on the dot so far. All I'm asking for is another week or two. Business is bound to pick up at the end of July. Then there are the bus tours I was telling you about—"

"You have a commitment from Le Bel Horizon? Something on paper you can show me?"

"Well, no. Not yet, but—"

"As well, there remains the problem of your competition. MacCallum Houseboats is still offering—um, barbecue cruises?"

"Yes," she faltered.

"*Je regrette, Mademoiselle Lowry.*" His face didn't look as though he regretted anything. "But head office determines the bank's policy. I can give you—and I am being generous—till Monday to meet the rest of your payment."

"Monday!"

"Otherwise—" he removed his spectacles and began polishing them "—I shall be obliged to ask you for a guarantor. Someone with the necessary collateral willing to cosign..."

Joy leaned back with a slow exhalation of breath. In a daze she gathered up her purse and umbrella, nodded at Monsieur Thierry, and let herself out of the bank. Why did she have that awful feeling that she'd been painted into a corner again?

CHAPTER TEN

SHE DROVE ALONG rue Principale, too numb to think. The only thing she knew for certain was that she had to get away, give her mind time to digest this latest blow and come up with a few answers before she went back to face the café. Opposite Raymond Frères on the out-skirts of town, instead of taking the road south around the lake, she flicked on her blinker and headed north, into the mountains.

She drove fast. It was a gravel road winding uphill through scrub and pasture land. Once this had been farming country, settled by sturdy French Canadian pioneers, but the stony soil, short summers and grind-ing winters made life hard for the *habitants*. Over the years, people had moved away, many of them into towns to make a living off the tourist trade, and the land retained a wild and lonely beauty. Trailing purple vetch and aromatic white yarrow bloomed along the road-side, dotted with the warm orange of devil's paint-brush. Just as Joy was rounding a bend in the road, the clouds lifted from the massive shoulder of a sprawling mountain, revealing a still higher peak. Mont Trem-blant, the highest peak in the Laurentian range: she re-alized suddenly she had been heading there all along. To find Rain, what else? Her unconscious mind had made the decision long before she dared even think about it.

Blue holes were opening up in the clouds by the time she reached Lac Supérieur. Wood-frame houses, neat and brightly painted as doll's houses, overlooked the lake, nestling amid steep hills of green-black spruce and maples that in September would burn with gold and crimson fire.

She had to brake hard, to avoid missing the turn-off to the road that skirted the north side of Mont Tremblant. What she was going to say to Rain, she had no idea; maybe, once again, her unconscious had already decided for her. The forests of Mont Tremblant Provincial Park crowded in on either side, spreading leafy canopies overhead. Magenta spires of fireweed swept the occasional clearing. A striped chipmunk scampered across the road, tiny tail erect as a banner. The sun came out and Joy rolled down her window to catch the scent of damp earth and moss. The Devil river, le Diable, raced alongside, boiling reddish brown over the rocks.

The road flattened and straightened, and she found herself at the southern foot of the mountain, with the long blue vista of Lac Tremblant spread out before her. To the right, picturesque as a postcard, the slope-roofed white and pastel cottages of Mont Tremblant Lodge climbed up to the ski lift. Higher still, cutting a rocky swathe through the timber, was the Flying Mile, the ski run that had made the mountain famous. And down there, somewhere, was Rain, she thought, heading the car toward a grove of masts rising from a sheltered arm of the lake. Her heart started to pound.

She parked the Honda and wandered down to the shore, wishing she'd worn other shoes than her high-heeled pumps. She might as well have, for all the good they'd done her with Monsieur Thierry. The boats on display were lined up along the docks of the marina; there were sailboats and dinghies and sleek fiberglass sailboards. A sizable crowd had assembled to inspect them; she'd need luck to catch sight of Rain. Booths had been set up along an improvised boardwalk, selling everything from yachting caps to life vests, as well as some tempting local crafts. Not that Joy had the heart to look at anything.

She strolled back and forth, on the lookout for one brown wind-tousled head looming above the rest, and feeling more and more forlorn. Music played over a loudspeaker system, the sun sparkled on the water, people chatted and laughed. It had never struck her before how many of them came in twos, how happy they looked with each other and how much they appeared to take their happiness for granted. She began to think she'd made a terrible mistake in coming. Rain could be anywhere: off with a client, or even on his way home by now. She felt drained and tired; she recalled that she'd been too nervous to eat lunch. At the end of the boardwalk was an open-air lunch counter, with tables set up under big gay umbrellas and fenced off by a cedar hedge. She'd have coffee, she decided, and then she'd leave.

She was searching in her handbag for her change purse and she didn't see the man at the counter ahead of her until he turned and they almost collided.

"Rain!"

"Joy!" She saw the look of surprise on his face turn to one of eager uncomplicated pleasure and felt a surge of happiness. Standing here on this unfamiliar lakeshore, in front of this tall bearded man in khaki slacks and an open-necked polo shirt, she had the craziest feeling of having come home.

"It's been a long week," he said softly.

"Yes." The last time they'd stood face to face had been Sunday, amid the debris of his possessions in front of her garage. She flushed.

"Who's minding the café?"

"Nobody."

"Don't tell me you took the afternoon off? Great! Have you seen the boats? Give me a minute and I'll show you around."

He sounded genuinely pleased, and keen as a boy. She wished despairingly that his version of the afternoon were the correct one. Quickly, before her confidence could ebb away any further, she blurted out, "I was at the bank this afternoon. I saw Monsieur Thierry about my mortgage payment."

"Did you?" Some of the light faded out of the coffee-brown eyes. "And?"

"I didn't have enough money. He gave me till Monday to come up with the rest. Otherwise, he says I have to find a guarantor."

"That's too bad." He watched her, waiting. The breeze blew a lock of his hair over his forehead. "What are you going to do?"

He was leaving it up to her. She was going to have to come right out and ask—not that she blamed him. She licked her dry lips and drew a breath. A couple of children ran up laughing to the counter. One of them jostled Rain's elbow. "Hey!" he yelled and did a quick juggling act to keep the contents of the plastic cups he was holding from sloshing over.

Two cups, she noticed. She'd been so busy with his eyes, his hands hadn't even registered.

"*P'tits gamins,*" he said, smiling at the children.

"I'm sorry to keep you," Joy began awkwardly. "I didn't realize you were . . . with someone."

"A client," he said smoothly and set the cups down on the counter. "Come on, I'll buy you a drink and then I'll introduce you to her."

Her? Joy's heart dipped. "No, really. I didn't mean to interrupt—"

"Soft drink? Coffee? I'm having a beer."

"Coffee, please. But—"

"*Un café, s'il vous plaît.* Is it written in stone somewhere that you've got to say black when I say white?" He put down the quarters and handed her the cup. "Come on. I was lucky enough to get a table."

It was off in the corner, next to the hedge. They'd almost reached it before she realized its other occupant was Miss Dark Hair from the party, who looked up as they approached. After a brief dismissive glance at Joy, she fixed smoky kohl-lined eyes on Rain.

"You took your time. I was beginning to think you'd lost interest."

"Lost interest? Never."

The woman laughed. She had a low throaty voice to match her sensuous French accent. She wore a stunning white jumpsuit that showed off her slender boyish figure. Joy wished herself invisible, or a hundred miles away. She'd been a fool to come. She should have known a man like Rain wasn't going to hang around waiting for her to change her mind. He'd made his offer and she had rejected it. If she came crying to him now for help, he'd know he was only second choice. Men like Rain weren't anybody's second choice, in anything. If there had been some way to keep from sitting down with them, she would have jumped at it. But under Rain's covert gaze, nothing plausible occurred to her. He made the introductions. "Danielle Demers, Joy Lowry. You two may have met at the party on Saturday."

"*Ah oui!* You are the girl who was having trouble with her boyfriend. That Paul what's-his-name. The one Rain threw in the lake."

"He was not my boyfriend. And Rain didn't throw him in." Face flushed, Joy went through the whole awkward explanation. Rain was no help. He sat nursing his beer with smug amusement stamped on his handsome features. She could have kicked him under the table except that, she reminded herself dolefully, she was in no position to kick anyone. A scratch pad covered with sketches of houseboat designs and columns of figures lay on the table. So at least the part about Danielle being a client was true. Rain caught her look.

"Danielle's father is buying her a houseboat. Something special."

"Very special. I plan to keep Rain very busy for a couple of months." She gave him a deep look from under half-lowered dark lashes. "Long enough so we can get to know each other really well."

"How nice, to have such a generous father," said Joy weakly.

"Generous? Papa?" Again the throaty laugh. "It is more a case of well trained. What Danielle wants, Danielle gets."

"Is that how you like your men?" Rain asked blandly. "Well trained?"

"That goes without saying. And you?" She rested delicate coral-tipped fingers on his bronzed forearm. "How do you like your women?"

Rain raised his arm to drink. "You'd be surprised," he said.

"Would I? Tell me about it."

Joy wondered if she'd become the victim of a strange new form of paralysis. She couldn't seem to get up from the chair. She couldn't even drink her coffee; it tasted like dishwater. She cleared her throat and said, much too loudly, "Do you live near here, Mademoiselle Demers?"

"When we're not in Montréal. Or Florida. We have a house just down the road in Mont Tremblant village." Her bored look vanished as she turned back to Rain. "Don't forget, you promised to come home with me."

"To inspect the site, sure."

"We could go in my Corvette and I'll drive you back here later. After supper. I know this little place..."

Joy got her muscles working; she put down her cup and rose unsteadily to her feet. "Well, I'll leave you to it. I have to get back to the café."

"Already?" said Rain. "Don't you want to see the boats?"

"I've seen enough," she said coldly. "Thanks for the coffee."

"Which you didn't drink. You never answered my question, either. What are you going to do about a guarantor?"

If he expected her to answer that in front of Miss Dark Hair, he was mistaken. She'd lose the cottage before she'd ask him to cosign now. "I'll think of something," she said. "Don't worry. I can see you have enough on your mind as it is."

His expression mocked her. "Only business. The usual. You know what it's like."

She flashed her eyes at him. "Business with Mademoiselle Demers, you mean."

"At least she has the sense to appreciate a good man when she sees one."

"Oh, really? Wait till those couple of months are up and she gets to know you! *Bonjour, mademoiselle.*" She spun on her heel. Rain pushed back his chair, but she didn't hear him get up. Instead she heard Danielle say something soft in French and giggle.

She didn't look back; she couldn't. Her heels beat a sharp staccato on the boardwalk. Everything around her looked extraordinarily vivid: the blue fiberglass hulls, the red metal roof of the little church snuggled between the pines, even the eyes of the people she passed. It was as though a pail of cold water had shocked everything to life. But she was the one who'd received the shock. She felt numb with humiliation.

The Honda was stifling in the late-afternoon sun. She rolled down the windows and switched on the radio, along with the ignition. Her favorite station was playing Vivaldi's *The Seasons*—the first good thing to have happened to her today. She turned up the volume and drove home in a fog of violins and misery.

THE SUNSET that evening was beautiful, as though nature were trying to make up for the way she felt.

A peach and amethyst glow in the west promised fine weather tomorrow. The water, too, had turned from gray to shades of amethyst. That was what she loved about Lac Désir, the way it mirrored every mood of sky and wind. For the first time it occurred to her that she might not be here much longer to see it. Her smile felt painted on as she served the handsomely dressed couple in the sun room.

"Delicious salad, my dear. I was just saying to George how fortunate we were to come across it again so soon. A local dish?"

Joy looked at the woman. "The ButterCup salad? You've eaten it somewhere else?"

"Yes. On the houseboat yesterday—we're thinking of buying one, you know. A lovely lunch, served by the prettiest young woman. It made up for the rain, didn't it, George? Artichoke hearts and hard-boiled eggs, cut to look like flowers. Perhaps you trade recipes?"

"Never," said Joy icily, sweeping up the plates. "A coincidence."

"Well!" said the woman. They left soon after, without ordering dessert or coffee.

It had to be Gipsy's doing. Joy had shown her how to make ButterCup salads just last week. Did Rain know about this? She remembered the truck had left late yesterday morning. He knew Gipsy couldn't cook; he must have guessed where the recipe came from. Maybe he'd even put her up to it. What was he planning to appropriate next?

The incident jolted her out of her dazed indecision. She scooped JS from the chair in the office and sat down to dial Montréal. Astonishing how the number sprang to mind, even though she hadn't called it in five months or more.

At the sound of Brian's voice, her own almost deserted her. "Hello, Brian? It's Joy. In Lac Désir."

"Joy. Well..." He sounded wary. "I was just on my way out. I'm attending a concert of that Russian pianist's. With Elinor," he said, pointedly.

"How nice for you. I just called to ask whether you'd have ten minutes' time for me at the office tomorrow."

There was a silence; this he clearly hadn't expected. "Possibly. Yes." His tone warmed. "Like to give me some idea what it's about?"

"I'd rather not say till I see you. Brian? It's very important to me."

"It must be," he said dryly. "To bring you into the city." He'd like to chat longer, he said, but Elinor hated to be kept waiting.

Her cheeks burned when she hung up. He'd put her properly in her place; but never mind, he was her last resort. Next on tonight's agenda was Gipsy, even if it meant staying up late. To pass the time, she went into the kitchen and baked a cinnamon pecan coffee cake. JS watched from the window seat, purring approval. His velvet ears pricked forward at the sound of the front door.

"Gipsy? Is that you?"

She put her head around the door, hair a careless handsome tangle. "Something smells good in here. Hi, Joy! Didn't know you were still up."

"I'm up and I'm furious. What are you trying to do? Sabotage the ButterCup?"

"Me? You're talking to me?"

"Yes, you. Bad enough you're working for Rain, but stealing my recipes for him is the absolute limit."

"Oh." Gipsy's hand shot guiltily to her mouth. "The ButterCup salad. How did you—? Listen, I didn't steal it. I just . . . remembered it."

"Give me a break!"

"Honestly. I never dreamed you'd take it like this. It's just that we were out of hot-dog rolls and I—"

"You never dreamed I'd find out, you mean."

"Well, that too. But there wasn't time to drive to the Supermarché and I looked in the cupboard, and there were these jars of artichoke hearts. Rain—"

"Don't tell me." Brusquely Joy tidied up the counter. "I don't want to know if Rain had anything to do with it. I don't think I could take it if he did."

The jade eyes were compassionate. "It's Monsieur Thierry, isn't it? He turned you down today."

"He gave me till Monday. But it's worse than that. I drove to Mont Tremblant to see Rain. To ask if he—oh Gipsy!" Something crumpled inside her. "He was with that dark-haired girl. Danielle Demers. And she was making a big play for him."

"That daddy's girl? Rain couldn't possibly fall for her. She's spoiled, selfish—"

"Pretty, sexy. And rich. She wants him to build her a custom houseboat."

Gipsy frowned and was silent. Men were her specialty, and experience hadn't given her much faith in them. She put out a comforting hand. "About the recipe. If it's any consolation, Rain was on the phone the whole morning about some windows that hadn't been delivered to a site. He didn't even see the salad. Believe me, it won't happen again."

Joy stored the cake under a glass bell; whatever had possessed her to bake something so unnecessary? She reached for the cat and tucked him under her arm. "Thanks, Gipsy," she said, mustering what dignity she could. At the foot of the stairs she looked back at her friend standing helpless in the doorway. "I almost forgot. A man phoned for you tonight. Long distance from Montréal."

"Did he leave his name?"

"No."

She slept badly. So did Gipsy; she heard her radio playing softly well into the night. She got up around two o'clock and went out on the balcony in her nightgown to stare over at the boat. She thought it might help to fill the aching void inside, but it didn't. The glow from Rain's bedroom skylight tinged the sky. She thought of him in his "Arabian Nights" hammock, not sleeping either.

"What a mess," she said into the dark. "What a stupid mess."

SHE ARRIVED at Lloyd & Upshaw's ten minutes early. The receptionist was new; Joy's name meant nothing to her.

"Miss Lowry, is it? Mr. Upshaw has a client with him now," she said. "Have a seat and I'll tell him you're here."

The rhododendron in the corner had put out two new leaves. The magazines on the table looked the same. The rumble of traffic on Dorchester, twenty-one floors down, vied with the hum of computers. She had spent five years of her life here, and now she had to fight an urge to bolt from the room.

Brian's door opened and the client left. One of the junior law partners recognized her and they exchanged a few words; afterward, she realized she had stared the whole time at his mustache because it reminded her of Rain's.

"Mr. Upshaw will see you now," said the receptionist. Another ten minutes had passed; Brian was putting her in her place again. He assessed her with cool gray eyes. She had lost faith in cream and mocha chic and was wearing a severe navy-blue linen suit. He made her feel as though she should have checked her lipstick and run a comb through her hair, but it was too late now. He indicated a chair and invited her to sit down.

"Well, Joy. Nice that you've finally found time to visit your old friends. Coffee?"

"Yes, please." Her mouth was dry. She waited while he went to the door and signaled the receptionist. His suit was an Italian summerweight, immaculately tailored. She could already tell he wasn't going to make this easy, but had she really expected otherwise? He listened without comment while she explained her situation at the bank. "What I came to ask, Brian, is would you sign as my guarantor?"

He pursed his lips. "And if I say no?"

"Brian, you wouldn't!" She struggled to recall the arguments she'd rehearsed on the drive down. "There's no risk. You know I'd pay you back. If worst comes to worst, I'll sell the cottage. As a simple kindness, Brian—"

"Would it be that?" He arched thin brows. "Maybe it would be kinder if I refused. Before you get in any deeper over your head."

She felt the color drain from her face. "You always wanted me to fail, didn't you? Right from the start."

He stiffened. "I didn't make it happen, Joy. I merely predicted it. You want some sound business advice? Sell the place now. To that roughneck MacCallum you seemed so keen on. He said he 'took an interest' in it—isn't that how he put it?"

An icy fury rose in her veins. "He's not a roughneck. And I don't want to sell the café to him or to anyone else. It would be like selling my dream! Besides, how would I make a living?"

"You always did tend to the melodramatic, didn't you? It's obvious. You'd come back to Montréal where you belong. I never told you this, but the girl filling your old position is only temporary. I'm sure Lloyd & Upshaw's could be persuaded to give the job back to you.''

She snatched up her handbag and rose to her feet. ''Give it to Elinor, why don't you? I can see I've made a terrible mistake by coming here and I certainly wouldn't want to make another.''

She closed the door with a firmness just short of a slam, brushed past the gaping receptionist holding two coffee cups, and rode trembling down the elevator. The tears didn't start until she stepped onto the pavement, into the blinding glare of the noonday sun. Fumbling in her bag for a handkerchief, she turned toward the parking garage and ran straight into Rain Mac-Callum's arms.

CHAPTER ELEVEN

"RAIN!" SHE GASPED, catching sight of his face through a blur of tears. She would have known him without looking by the hard muscular feel of him, the woodsy fresh-shirt scent, in the split second before she stepped hastily back. "What . . . what are you doing here?"

"Waiting for you."

"I don't understand. How did you—" her breath caught in a sob "—know where I'd be?"

"Gipsy told me you were driving down to see Upshaw." He shrugged, arms at his sides. "So I looked up lawyers in the Yellow Pages." He didn't try to hold her. She felt intimidated by his light fawn suit. She had never seen him in a suit before. Combined with the neat trim beard and combed-back hair, it gave him an air of urbane distinction—as though he worked on the twenty-first floor. No, she amended with a silent pang—as though he owned the building. A Cadillac trying to exit the garage honked irritably and they moved aside.

"I broke the speed limit getting here. I thought I could still catch you in time," he said.

"In time?" Traffic roared ceaselessly along Dorchester, making it difficult to hear.

"Don't pretend. In time before you asked Brian Upshaw to be your guarantor. I take it the great man said no?"

"How did you—" She stopped; there was no earthly reason for her to feel so guilty about it. "Are you here to gloat?"

The ghost of a smile passed over his face. "Is it obligatory?" She hadn't realized how strained he looked. His hand on her elbow steered her into the garage. "Come on. We'll talk over lunch."

She wished insanely that he'd put his arm around her. "I don't think I could eat."

"Wait till you see this little place I know in Old Montréal. We'll ask for a table under the vine leaves. Besides, what I have to tell you will restore your appetite."

It was like a dream that he should be here with her. Why, didn't matter. They took the Honda instead of the truck because it would be easier to park. The restaurant wasn't far, only a few blocks down Beaver Hall Hill and then left along rue Saint Paul to a low stone house with a view of the old Mariners' church. The door was oak and carved with the fleur-de-lis emblem of New France, the chips and scars of age lovingly polished. Rain had to duck his head to pass under the lintel. Inside was the dim cool world of two centuries ago. Oak beams supported the ceiling, copper pots filled with fresh flowers hung in an open hearth, the tables were laid with handwoven catalogne cloth. Rain spoke to someone, and they found themselves in a stone courtyard dappled with sunlight filtering greenly through a trellis of vine leaves. Rain pulled out her chair. In the diffused undersea light, the lines in his face softened.

"A drink?" he asked, and without waiting for an answer, ordered two Dubonnets on the rocks with twists of lemon. They opened mock parchment menus. Surreptitiously, she used her handkerchief.

"He's not worth your tears," Rain said.

"I know that!" she flared. It wasn't quite noon and they had the courtyard to themselves except for some sparrows pecking at crumbs. "I feel so humiliated. All I wanted was his signature."

"Nothing else?"

"What else do you think I wanted from him?"

He raised a square shoulder, let it drop. He wore an off-white shirt and a silk tie handsomely patterned in brown and gold that picked up the tints in his eyes and hair. "It's academic, what I think," he said. "See anything you like on the menu?"

"Oh." She hadn't even looked. "A salad of some kind."

"That's it?" He frowned. "Listen, it's an insult for a woman to starve herself when a man takes her out to lunch. You'll have crêpes as well. Chicken or seafood?"

"Seafood," she snapped. She waited until the waitress, a pretty girl in periwinkle blue with a laced bodice and a frilled cap, had taken their order. "What do you mean, it's academic?"

The sudden bitterness in his glance shocked her. "Isn't it obvious? It's Upshaw you went to. Not me."

"But that's because..." Her voice trailed away, as a whole new vista opened before her. Rain, jealous? Hurt? Mesmerized, she watched as he extracted a piece of paper from his wallet and slapped it, face up, on the table. "Read it," he barked.

She picked it up. In spite of the hot July day, she felt a chill run down her back. It was a contract with a trucking firm for the transportation of a houseboat from Lac Désir to Lac des Sables. "But that's...for La

Grosse Grenouille. Rain—" She looked up, disbelieving. "You're not having your boat moved?"

"Boat, house, head office. Demo cruises, barbecues, late nights, litter, racket. The whole shooting match." She gaped at him. Noisily the bells pealed twelve o'clock across the street and hearing became impossible. But it didn't matter; she couldn't find the words anyway. He looked impatient.

"Don't you understand?" He drained his glass and leaned forward. "You've won! MacCallum Houseboats is leaving. Everything on the beach will be the way it was before. Well, close..."

"But...Lac Désir is your home."

"I thought there was room for both of us, that we could work something out. But—" he looked away, though not quickly enough to hide the bleakness in his eyes "—it seems not. Lac des Sables is bigger, more central, with a larger tourist population. From a business standpoint, it's a good move."

The waitress put down their plates.

"There's more to life than business," Joy heard herself say feebly. Coming from her, it sounded like a joke.

Rain, reaching for his fork, gave a short laugh. "Poor kid. I hope so. I haven't made it easy for you, have I?" He winced at the look on her face. "Listen, in spite of what you think, it was never my intention to force you out of business. Sure, I want the cottage. But not if it means you losing the café. When you turned down my partnership offer, I started looking for an alternate berth. It took a while; not everybody wants a big green houseboat parked off their beach. As you know..." He stopped, frowning. "You're not eating."

"Neither are you." It was true; he'd put down his fork and pushed his plate aside. He gave a wry grin and signaled the waitress for coffee. "Okay. Okay. You win that one, too." He sat back, the shadow of the vine leaves playing across his features. "Well, aren't you going to say something?"

She wished he'd stop saying she won. She felt like the ultimate loser. "When are you . . . when are they coming to move you?"

"Tomorrow. I meant, say something else."

Tomorrow already. "Like what?"

"Like fantastic! About time! Good riddance!"

"No," she said in a small voice, watching the waitress pour coffee into blue-and-white cups and put cream on the table in a china pitcher fat as one of the sparrows. That wasn't what she wanted to say at all. She clutched at straws. "What about the wharf? All the money and effort you put into it . . ."

"You use it. Get yourself a boat." He raised eloquent eyebrows. "A rowboat."

She felt the tears pricking at the back of her eyes. The tables were filling up around them. Tourists in colorful shirts and slender secretaries, vivacious and pretty as only French women could be, a sprinkling of executives in suits like Rain's. She stared into her cup.

"Why are you doing this? I mean the real reason. You're a businessman. You have as much right to conduct your business on your own property as I have. Why should you care if I can't take the competition? Especially—" she drew a deep breath "—when you stand to benefit in the end?"

He took the check the waitress placed on the table between them, scanned it, and put down some bills. "Can't you guess?" he said.

They walked through the dim, cool dining room out onto the sunlit sidewalk. Beside the courtyard wall, where the Honda was parked, he turned, his hair a russet halo. His eyes met hers, full and frank, and the answer in them nearly bowled her over. Her mouth went dry and she had trouble breathing. He couldn't mean what she was reading. But then he said out loud, in a clear soft voice, "I fell in love with you, Joy. Why else?"

"Oh. Oh, Rain. All this time I thought..." What was it Clémence had said? *The greatest gift in the world, love. And we are so afraid of presenting it to one another.* "Why didn't you tell me?" she asked in anguish.

"I did. Several times, the best way I knew how." He unlocked the passenger door for her and waited. "Would the words have made any difference? You were so convinced I was out to ruin the ButterCup and get my hands on the cottage. Don't say it!" He held up his hand as he maneuvered himself into the driver's seat. "I know. Men have been known to make love for less. Well, I'm not that kind of guy. If you don't know that yet—forget it."

She felt like a swimmer buffeted by conflicting tides. "Rain. Maybe it's too late, but I have to tell you—" How? Where to start? Already he had the engine in gear and was heading up Beaver Hall Hill. The windows were open because the car had been standing in the sun, and the entire roar and rumble of downtown traffic seemed to be funneling in. A car horn blared behind them, a taxi cut in front; Rain swore. At the intersection an ambulance went wailing north against the light. They turned into the Dorchester street garage and she still hadn't managed to get a word out. He left the motor running.

"You'll make it back all right from here? To the autoroute?"

"Rain, wait, please!" She got out when he did and came around the hood of the car. She couldn't believe this was how it was going to end, in a parking garage next to Lloyd & Upshaw's glass and concrete tower. "I haven't told you yet—"

He had the key to the truck in his hand and the impatient look back on his face. "You don't have to thank me, if that's what's bothering you. Gratitude's the last thing I want from you."

A car honked behind them, waiting for the Honda's parking spot.

"I don't want to thank you!" she shouted. "Damn you, Rain MacCallum. I'm telling you I love you!"

For an instant she thought she was getting through to him. Then his expression changed. "It's all right. You don't have to try and make me feel better. The ButterCup's safe." He swung his limber frame up into the truck's cab and wound down the window. His grin under the mustache was lopsided, not a real grin at all. "Come Monday you'll be laughing in Thierry's face. You'll see. That's what you really wanted all along."

"It isn't! Not anymore. It's you—" But it was too late. He was already backing out, already leaving. The waiting car almost ran her down. Her shoulders slumped as she stepped into the Honda.

The drive back to Lac Désir was the longest of her life. In the rearview mirror the green crown of Mont Royal, lapped by the city and topped by its landmark steel cross, took forever to recede into the horizon. Last to fade were the copper dome of Saint Joseph's Oratory and the yellow building-block towers of l'Université de Montréal. Ahead, the Laurentians were faint charcoal etchings in a sky bleached colorless by the July sun.

Over and over her mind replayed the words Rain had said. How could she have been so blinded by fear—fear of losing the café, the cottage, her dream? Well, she'd saved them, and in the process she'd lost Rain. The irony of it was in realizing too late that without him, the rest meant nothing to her.

As Joy pushed wearily through the screen door, Madame Hebert turned a relieved face from the zucchini boats she was taking out of the oven.

"Ah, Mademoiselle Lowry! I was worried. You said two o'clock, and it is nearly five." She clucked sympathetically. "Come, sit down. I have made iced tea."

Joy's tears almost started afresh at this offering of kindness from an unexpected source. "I . . . was invited to lunch and then I got caught in the traffic. Friday afternoon . . ." she gestured helplessly. And the last two weeks in July: half of Montréal had been streaming north on the autoroute.

"Already they are phoning for reservations. I told Lisette she must come." Madame Hebert slid the boats smoothly out of the pan. "When you do not arrive, I think, we will serve *un dîner végétarien*. It is—"

"All we can afford. I know." Joy smiled wanly and sipped her tea, making the ice cubes tinkle. "A good idea. But do you think there'll be that many people?"

"Mais oui." The older woman gave her a quick unreadable glance. "Monsieur MacCallum has canceled the evening cruise."

Of course. She'd seen the truck just now, parked at the end of the wharf. He and Yves would be battening down the hatches or whatever it was they did when houseboats took to the road. Joy finished her tea in heavy-hearted silence, even though Madame Hebert was no doubt waiting for her to volunteer her comments. She didn't even want to think about it, much less speak. "Dessert," she mused, with her head in the refrigerator. "What can I make in ten minutes with a lot of milk and a few eggs? Something I can give a catchy title to..."

"Coffee Floating Island," declared Madame Hebert in English that sounded like French, and Joy was relieved to have the decision taken from her.

She needn't have worried about thinking. There wasn't time. Word spread like a forest fire that La Grenouille was leaving, and tourists and local people alike seemed determined to crowd into the ButterCup for a farewell view over supper. Joy had three sittings and was still turning them away. She ran out of everything except bread and coffee but it didn't seem to matter. The sunset, behind the hulking green frog ablaze with lights, was one of nature's most spectacular. Well after midnight Joy reeled up to bed and against all her expectations, fell instantly asleep.

She awoke to the shriek of wrenching nails. It was barely seven. Had he been up all night? She padded across to the balcony, holding her head. She felt as though she had a hangover, but it was just a deep and pervading sense of misery. The night had been relatively cool, and coils of mist rose undulating like wraiths from the still surface of the lake, their upper reaches tinged with golden light. Rain was removing the flower boxes. His powerful wrist flexed and straightened, wielding the claw hammer; there was no joy in his movements this morning.

"Rain, stop!" she wanted to shout. "Don't go. I love you." She wrapped her arms around herself to keep from shivering. How could she convince him? There had to be a way.

Like a zombie she wandered into the bathroom. After last night's take, Monsieur Thierry should have been chortling with glee. Instead he looked the way she felt. She pulled an old cotton sundress over her head and pushed her fingers through her hair. On the landing, she paused. Gipsy's door was ajar. The room was empty, the bed made up and strewn with the clothes she'd tried on and rejected yesterday. Gipsy hadn't come home last night.

Helping Rain? Maybe even consoling him? Joy fought off the clawing suspicions all the way down the stairs and hated herself for them.

She plugged in the coffee maker, dished out some cat food for JS, and wandered through the cool empty rooms, mug in hand. The geraniums needed watering and the tablecloths changing. On the desk, in yesterday's mail, she discovered a postcard from California. Her father, writing in his long-ago spidery hand to thank her for her letter: he was touched, he said, and very proud to think of her success. He'd be traveling to Canada with a friend in September, and they would be sure to stop for lunch at the ButterCup.

"Well," she thought, with the breath knocked out of her. She sat down in the kitchen and pulled the recipe file toward her. It was no use; she felt sick. She wasn't going to cook today. Rain, Rain, it beat in her brain. The café was just a marathon ordeal, the source of all her troubles. She laid her head on her arms and let the tears flow.

"Joy? Are you there?" Gipsy burst into the kitchen, eyes shining, hair loose over her shoulders. "Joy! The most fabulous news!"

Joy frowned blurrily. "Gipsy! Where have you been?"

"That's the news! I've been with Bruno. He tracked me down to the houseboat yesterday and kidnapped me. He absolutely insisted we drive somewhere for dinner and to—well, spend the night. Joy, darling! His wife's agreed to a divorce. Bruno and I are going to be married!"

"Oh," said Joy. She fumbled a napkin out of the holder and blew her nose. "How wonderful. I'm so glad for you."

"Joy, what is it? You look ghastly. You've been crying." She bent to give her a hug. "Brian turned you down, is that it?"

"No. I mean yes, he turned me down. But I don't care, it's not that. Gipsy, Rain is leaving. Moving the houseboat to Lac des Sables."

Her friend stared, struck speechless for once, and Joy got to her feet. "I'm sorry, putting a damper on your news like this. Never mind Rain for now. Where is Bruno?"

"Outside in the car. I just came back to tell you, and to collect my things so I can drive back to Montréal with him. But I can't leave you like this—"

"Yes, you can. It's my problem and you'd only complicate things. Can I meet this dream man of yours? Ask him in for a coffee?"

"Joy, would you? I'd love the two of you to meet. Bruno's a teddy bear—you'll see."

He was, too, noted Joy in surprise; nothing like her idea of a big-name television producer. A short round man, the kind you could hug, with a bald spot on the top of his head. Not handsome, but he had a warm intelligent smile and a kind voice. Wrong twice in two days about a man, she thought, making small talk and busying herself with the coffee so he wouldn't see too much of her eyes. He sat in the window seat, with JS purring around him, openly appreciative of the hospitality and the chance to sing Gipsy's praises. Maybe the two of them did have a chance together, thought Joy, as Gipsy bumped down the stairs with her cases and he sprang to help.

"Promise to call? Let me know what you're going to do?" Gipsy squeezed her hand in the dim foyer. "Thanks for everything, and I hope you understand. Now that Bruno's found me again, I can't bear to spend another minute away from him. I'd follow him to the North Pole, if he asked."

To the North Pole, or to the next lake—if you loved someone, following him was the natural thing to do. As she waved goodbye from the porch, the thought that had been taking timid root at the back of her mind ever since she awoke burst into full bloom.

She pulled the telephone across the reception desk and dialed. Nine o'clock, and outside the mists had burned away to reveal shimmering waves reflecting a china-blue sky. On a day like this the Laurentians would be swarming with people looking for cottages. "Clémence? Can you come over right away? With a For Sale sign and the necessary papers?"

"*C'est toi,* Joy? Or is this a bad dream?"

It took a few minutes to convince her. "I'll explain when you get here. Oh, and one other thing. Do you know of any houses for sale on Lac des Sables?"

"It's not my territory, but I could pass the office on my way and find out..."

"Clémence, you're an angel! Can you make it soon?"

"Just as soon as I have my coffee and do my face."

In less than an hour, the little red sportscar rumbled into the parking lot. At the sight of the For Sale sign propped up on the passenger seat, Joy let out the breath she seemed to have been holding since the phone call. Trust Clémence not to let her down. Mouth dry with apprehension, she held open the door. Silhouetted against the sky, the Viking was hauling down the fleur-de-lis. The railings were bare and the awnings had all been rolled back, giving the boat a plundered look. Even the little birdhouses were gone. Grabber, nose on his paws, lay forlornly on the wharf next to a jumble of cartons.

Climbing out of the car with her briefcase in hand, Clémence cast a wry glance over her shoulder. "The whole town is talking of nothing else. The mayor is thinking of sending a deputation to ask him to change his mind." She turned to Joy. "No need to explain, *ma petite*. I am devastated it had to come to this. But in your shoes I would do the same."

In twenty minutes' time they had agreed on a figure, Joy had signed the papers, and Clémence had gone over a partial listing of the smaller houses for sale on Lac des Sables with her. "I left a note for Jacques—he's the realtor for that area. Now, the sign. The sooner we put it up, the better. Am I right?"

They dug it into the marigold bed, where it couldn't help but catch the eye. Clémence's manner was almost brusque. "It is too soon for goodbyes, *ma petite*. And no matter what, we will remain friends, *d'accord?*"

"D'accord," said Joy huskily. When she came back inside, she was engulfed by the most awful sense of desolation. Now she knew what people meant by burning their bridges. The trouble was, she didn't know what

lay on the other side. Maybe she was making the biggest mistake of her life. Even the silence held an accusing sound. She put the second Brandenburg concerto, the most rousing of the six, in the cassette player and turned up the volume. She was upstairs, sorting out drawers, when somebody hammered on the front door. Prospective clients already, she thought wildly, and skimmed down the stairs.

Rain stood outside, in work boots and jeans. One look at his eyes and she shivered. "Don't you *care* anymore?" he rumbled.

He held out a cupped hand and she caught the glint of bright button eyes and an upthrust beak. She gasped. Sheltered in his palm was a baby robin with a downy speckled breast. "Another split second, and JS would have had him in his jaws. Any idea where the nest is?"

"Yes." She pulled herself out of the heady daze his nearness was causing. "In the lilacs at the back."

She walked beside him over the dewy morning grass with her yellow skirt swinging about her knees, scarcely daring to breathe in case he disappeared. She indicated the nest, concealed just above their heads, and watched as he reached up from his superior height and deftly tipped the youngster in to join his siblings. The robin couple swooped up, sounding Red Alert.

"Come on," yelled Rain, grabbing her hand and racing to the back door with her, the birds shrieking and diving in hot pursuit.

"Cats!" he declared, putting his entire opinion into the word.

"He's only doing what Grabber does. If you recall." The screen door banged behind them. "Is that what you came over to complain about?"

He looked taken aback, then recovered his frown. "No, as a matter of fact. It was your loud music."

"Bach?"

"I don't care who it was. I could hardly hear the ten-thirty news. Then I saw the For Sale sign. Is that supposed to be some kind of *joke*?"

"No. I'm selling the cottage," she said innocently.

"What the hell for? Now that you've won. Now that you've got the entire lake to yourself."

"It's nice of you to keep saying I won." She was amazed at the calmness of her tone when her heart was doing a mile a minute. "Coffee?" she asked. "Actually, I found out I lost."

"Lost?" he echoed warily. He sank onto the window seat, while she got out mugs and poured. "Good grief, woman, what more is there? I bent over backward. I've given in..."

"Have you?" She couldn't bring herself to look at him. His mere presence in the kitchen was enough to send messages tingling up and down her spine. Her eye fell on the cinnamon pecan coffee cake and she removed the bell and set it on the table. "Cake?" she asked, and began slicing. "Hasn't it occurred to you that maybe there's something I wanted a great deal more than the café?" She handed him the plate. "If you're still interested in the cottage, I'm sure Clémence would welcome a call."

"And you?" His voice was suddenly quiet and aware. "What will you do?"

"Depends on how much I get for the cottage." She threw him a sidelong glance. "A *patates frites* wagon might be fun. I could park it on a beach."

"You could." He helped himself to another wedge of cake. It had turned out flawlessly: moist, rich, fragrant. "Any special location in mind?"

She smiled. "I hear Lac des Sables is nice. Bigger, more central, a larger tourist population. A good move from a business standpoint."

His upper lip twitched under the mustache. "Anything else?"

"Yes." Her smile trembled ever so slightly. "I hear there's lots of competition at Lac des Sables. I sort of got used to that this summer."

His eyes danced. "I know the feeling. On the other hand, you can't beat Lac Désir for beauty. It's the up-and-coming place. If lack of competition bothers you, a couple of phone calls could fix that in nothing flat."

"You mean, back to the impasse?" His eyes were making her bold. "Is that wise?" She sipped her coffee and pretended to think. "Maybe if I took on a partner..."

"Yes?"

"Somebody I know and can trust. Somebody who could use my expertise in cooking. And a half share in the cottage."

Rain expelled a long explosive breath. "Why didn't you come to me earlier? Instead of going to Thierry? And yesterday to Brian Upshaw?"

"How could I? When I didn't know how you felt about me? When I thought you were after the cottage? It would have been too painful." She raised her head. "Besides, I did come to you. You were busy with Miss Dark Hair."

"Who?"

"At Mont Tremblant. Danielle. The one who wants a houseboat."

"Oho! The man-eater!" He shrugged. "I told her to forget it. I don't do custom work in the bedrooms. Not for clients."

She flushed. "Why did you let me think—"

"I did, didn't I? Maybe because I was hurt, angry." His voice dropped and he looked at her. "Because I didn't know how you felt about *me . . .*"

Their eyes connected. She thought the room had suddenly tilted. He rose to his feet and came around the table. "Joy, oh Joy," he murmured, holding out his arms for her to move into. "I had to be sure. Just like you." He rocked her back and forth, rubbing his cheek on the springy top of her head. She felt the broad solid warmth of him, the beat of his heart, his soft curly chin on her forehead.

"Be sure," she whispered. "I am." She took his hand and pressed his callused palm against her warm cheek. "I love you, Rain," she said, out loud and at last unafraid.

He held her away from him and his eyes kindled dark fires in her veins. "I don't know what I would have done, if you hadn't found a way to convince me. Given up the business and gone back to the Fraser, maybe. Joy, I went through hell this past week, thinking I was leaving here without you." He drew her close, as though every second apart from her was one too many. "I'm going to make sure it never happens again."

"Really?" she said, feeling the familiar warmth spread through her. "How?"

"There's another kind of partnership. The kind that's sealed with a ring and if we're lucky, lasts a lifetime." He paused, his tone husky. "Will you marry me, Joy?"

"I . . . I'd need persuading. Do you have means?"

"Do you doubt it?" His brows rose wickedly. "I'd start with a pleasure dome. Add a hammock and a couple of Closed signs." He pulled her tight against him. "I'd tell you I loved you. And then I'd do this." He tipped back her head. "And this." He brought his lips down on hers and slowly, irresistibly, tenderly, heaven opened its doors for her.

She gave a sigh of pure bliss. Outside on the front porch, Grabber whined politely. She thought of JS somewhere out there, and then she relaxed.

JS would have to take his chances, just as she had.

EPILOGUE

JOY AND RAIN would like to share with you some of the recipes that highlighted their romance.

Sample the ButterCup salad that nearly brought about the end of their relationship in Chapter 10 because Joy thought Rain had stolen the recipe from her. On a festive occasion, you might like to try the maple charlotte served by Joy in Chapter 2 when opening night at the Café had to compete with the construction of Rain's wharf across the road. Later on, share with someone special a glass of the Russian tea Rain brewed for Joy in Chapter 5, and dream a few Arabian Nights dreams of your own.

As Joy and Rain found out, food and drink can be forces for division, but they can be even greater forces for love. They invite you and your family to join in this discovery.

BUTTERCUP SALAD FOR TWO

  l large tomato, cut in chunks
  ¼ English cucumber, thinly sliced & quartered
  2 green onions, chopped
  l small (6¼ oz.) jar marinated artichoke hearts
  l egg, hard boiled
  lettuce leaves

Salt, freshly ground pepper, celery salt (optional)
dash of lemon juice

Drain artichoke hearts, and set the marinade
aside. Arrange the tomato, cucumber, onion & artichoke hearts in a bowl; season lightly to taste.
Whisk the marinade with a fork until creamy and
pour over the salad. Cover and chill for 1 hour.

Cut the hard-boiled egg in half crosswise. With
a sharp-tipped knife, cut a zigzag pattern in the egg
white to form petals around the yolk. Toss the
salad lightly, add lemon juice to taste, and serve on
lettuce leaves, arranged on individual plates. Garnish each serving with half an egg, seasoned to
taste.

Makes 2 servings.

Good with toast points.

MAPLE CHARLOTTE

1 tbsp. unflavored gelatine
¼ cup cold water
¾ cup maple syrup
1 pint 35% cream, whipped
ladyfingers
½ cup toasted almond slivers

Sprinkle the gelatine over cold water and let
soften. Heat the maple syrup and add the gelatine
mixture until it dissolves. Cool until it thickens
(enough to coat a spoon). Whip the cream until
stiff and fold it into the gelatine-syrup mixture.

Line a glass bowl with ladyfingers and pour in the cream mixture. Chill 4 hours (or until firm).

Unmold and garnish with the toasted almond slivers.

Makes eight servings.

RAIN'S RUSSIAN TEA

Make a pot of strong tea.

Place 1 tsp. raspberry, strawberry or cherry preserve (jam will do fine) in each glass or pottery mug. Add piping-hot tea and garnish with a paper-thin slice of lemon.

Six exciting series for you every month... from Harlequin

Harlequin Romance
The series that started it all

Tender, captivating and heartwarming...
love stories that sweep you off to faraway places
and delight you with the magic of love.

◆

Harlequin Presents

Powerful contemporary love
stories...as individual as the
women who read them

The No. 1 romance series...
exciting love stories for you, the woman of today...
a rare blend of passion and dramatic realism.

◆

Harlequin Superromance®
It's more than romance...
it's Harlequin Superromance

A sophisticated, contemporary romance-fiction
series, providing you with a longer,
more involving read...a richer mix of complex plots,
realism and adventure.

Harlequin
American Romance™
Harlequin celebrates the American woman...

...by offering you romance stories written about American women, by American women for American women. This series offers you contemporary romances uniquely North American in flavor and appeal.

◆

Harlequin Temptation™
Passionate stories for today's woman

An exciting series of sensual, mature stories of love...dilemmas, choices, resolutions... all contemporary issues dealt with in a true-to-life fashion by some of your favorite authors.

◆

Harlequin Intrigue™
Because romance can be quite an adventure

Harlequin Intrigue, an innovative series that blends the romance you expect... with the unexpected. Each story has an added element of intrigue that provides a new twist to the Harlequin tradition of romance excellence.

Harlequin Books™

PROD-A-2